SIX MURDERS?

The strange case of The Welly Alley Strangler

By
Robert Philip Bolton

Also by Robert Philip Bolton

The Fine Art of Kindness
Underneath The Arclight
To The White Gate
My Marian Year
The Boltons of The Little Boltons
The Tapu Garden of Eden
Nana's Special Day and other stories
The Dolphin and other stories
Quickies
The Collected Short Stories
For Viktor. The story of Mussorgsky's 'Pictures at an Exhibition'

AUTHOR'S NOTE: *Six Murders?* is a work of fiction and the characters it depicts are the products of my imagination. Any resemblance to any real person living or dead is therefore entirely coincidental.

Robert Philip Bolton was born in New Zealand in 1945. He has been writing most of his adult life. Most of his work is about New Zealand and New Zealanders. He lives in Auckland.

THE STRANGE CASE OF THE WELLY ALLEY STRANGLER
By
Robert Philip Bolton
Cover by Stephen Bolton
Copyright © Robert Philip Bolton (v2 07/19)
ISBN: 978-0-473-39101-0

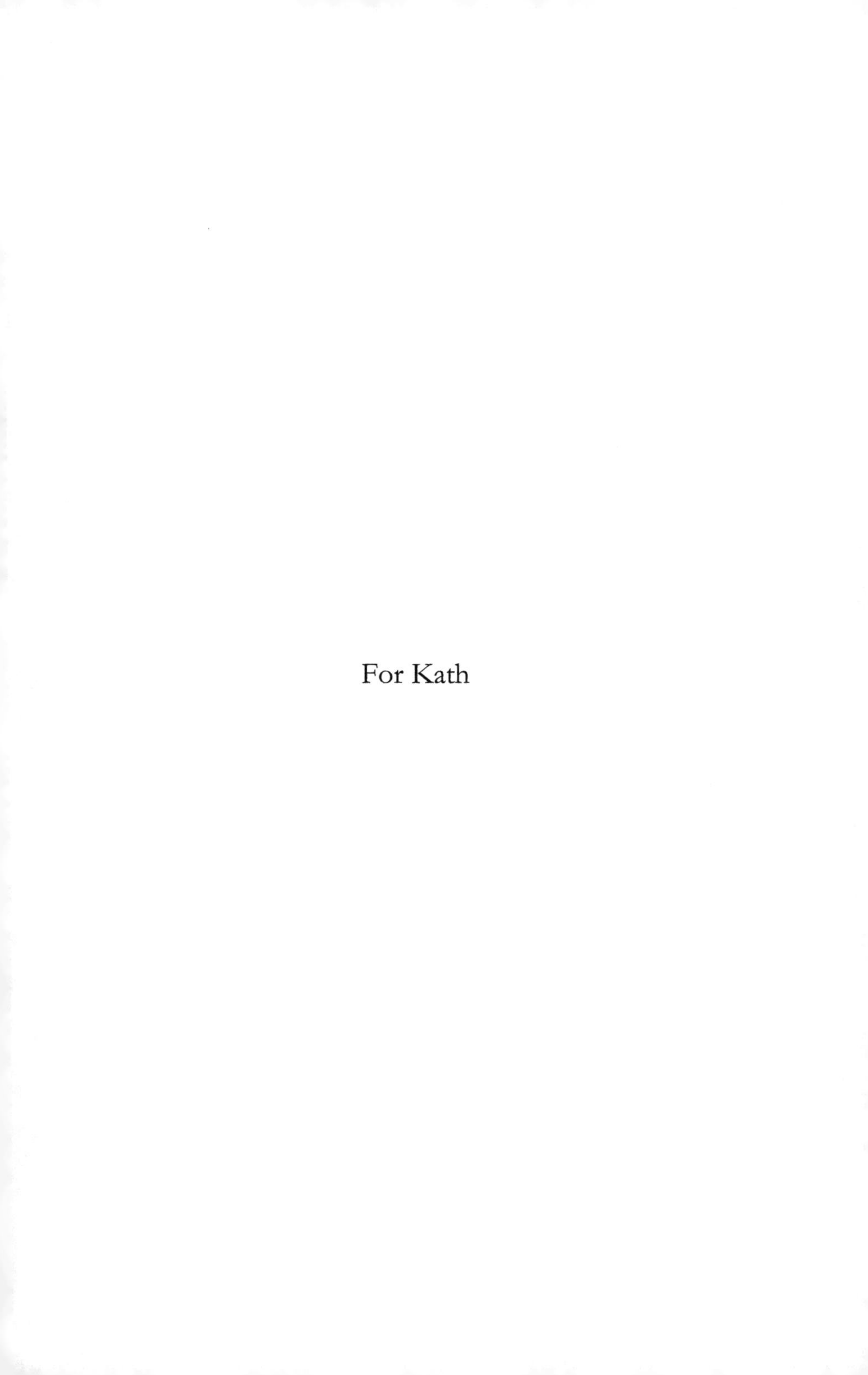

For Kath

PART ONE

Chapter 1

'Benjamin Cedric Pye, you have been found guilty of assault with intent to injure Sione Edward Christian, a good and innocent person going about his work honestly and earnestly, on the evening of the first of October this year.' At this point the judge paused and, looking over the top of her reading spectacles, added sternly: 'Look at me as I address you please, Mr Pye.'

At this point the guilty Pye man was guilty of looking to the back of the number one permanent criminal court and grinning evilly at two dull-looking young men – hardly more than teenagers – who were sitting together grinning evilly back. The guilty Pye man, holding his humourless smile, slowly and arrogantly turned his gaze back to the front of the court and to the severe-looking lady judge who was still humourlessly looking down at him from the bench over the top of her spectacles.

'Listen to me now, Mr Pye,' continued The Honourable Justice Dame Alexandrina Prohm, OBE, the principal judge of the number one permanent criminal court of Wellington. 'Due to the severe nature and extent of the injuries to Mr Christian caused by your actions that terrible evening it is my duty–' (she wanted to say "it is my delicious pleasure, you evil prick" but didn't) '—to impose the maximum sentence allowed by law. You are therefore sentenced by this court to imprisonment for thirty-six months. You will now be removed from this place, taken down to the cells and thence to Te Whareherehere prison where you will remain confined at Her Majesty's pleasure for the duration of your sentence.'

Thus was sentence grimly passed on a grinning Benjamin Cedric Pye by the principal judge of the number one permanent criminal court in her gloomy Wellington court-room on that otherwise bright December afternoon. And when it was pronounced, and before he was led away to the basement cells by the C and C security guards, whence he would be transported to Te Whareherehere prison – known by its inmates, exmates, employees, visitors (official and otherwise), journalists, politicians and others, indeed by everyone in Wellington, as The Lake – for the duration of his sentence, the said Benjamin Cedric Pye, a huge man now gone somewhat to fat, a former heavy-weight boxer known for the mighty power behind his punches and the great size of his meaty fists, with wrists so thick that no handcuffs could be found large enough to encircle them, merely looked again to the back of the court, to the two young thugs, from whom any shred of gorm they might once have possessed had long since departed, dressed unfashionably alike in their tight black trousers, black vinyl jackets, black heeled boots and white open-neck shirts, and grinned evilly at them again.

'He looks happy as a fart,' said Eric the Limp, the taller and spottier of the two young apprentice thugs, to his shorter and squatter companion as they made ready to leave the court.

'He shouldn't be,' said Tatts McIndoe, the short round one. 'Thirty-six months.'

'How much is that in real proper years?' asked Eric the Limp.

'Thirty-six months, my brother,' said Tatts McIndoe, 'equals three years. Three whole years in The Lake.'

'Then why's he so farting cheerful?' asked Eric the Limp.

'Why indeed, brother?' said his brother. 'Why indeed?'

Twelve days later, that being Christmas day, the two obnoxious and gormless young brothers Tatts McIndoe and Eric the Limp, seen together in court at the sentencing of Big Ben Pye – for that is how he was known in the Wellington underworld and beyond – were standing together beside the concrete plinth of one of the six great fluted pillars which stand majestically at the front of the Metropolitan Cathedral of the Sacred Heart and of Saint Mary His Mother, better known locally as Sacred Heart Cathedral, on Hill Street. They were with another young man – a big man, as big as Big Ben but much younger – known simply as Simple Simon. Simple Simon towered over his two companions whom he made look not merely small but weak, weedy and pasty-faced. Indeed, Simple Simon was not only as big and bulky as the recently incarcerated for three years Big Ben Pye – with whom, by associating with him recently, and with some of his associates, during a couple of brief terms in Te Whareherehere, he had become well acquainted – but was also considerably younger, healthier, stronger and fitter than the older man although evidently only marginally more intelligent; and he was certainly better looking which wasn't necessarily a great accomplishment as Big Ben was noted for an ugliness of appearance to complement the gross ugliness of his nature.

'There is two-and-a-half thousand there now, my friend and ally,' said Tatts McIndoe with faux ceremony as he handed

Simple Simon a plastic Countdown shopping bag. 'Do you understand?' he added slowly, carefully enunciating each word.

'Get on with it, Tatts,' said Eric the Limp quietly, impatiently, to his shorter brother. He was looking nervously at the moving line of incoming Christmas morning worshippers passing them in the narrow passage to the main door. 'He's not your friend or whatsiname. And don't forget, he's thick as pig shit. Why waste time on him?'

This blunt and coarse communication from brother to brother was not what one would expect to hear in the portico of a Roman Catholic cathedral on a Christmas morning while preparations were being made within for the celebration of Holy Mass; but it did occur, is germane, and thus must be reported.

'Be quiet, Limpy, I beg of you,' said Tatts McIndoe as loudly as he dared. And then – the Countdown shopping bag having been officially transferred – he said to the said Simple Simon, slowly, in a dreary monotone, as if speaking to a rather dull child: 'Big Ben said that you know what to do and that you shall receive the balance when he receives confirmation that you have completed the contract satisfactorily on new year's eve precisely as arranged and understood by parties of the both parts.'

'Eh?' said Simple Simon as he dropped his missal into the shopping bag with the money.

'It's a down payment, cockhead,' said Eric the Limp. He reached up – and despite his own tallness he did have to reach up – and gripped Simple Simon's crookedly-tied paisley tie, looked up at him, and he really did have to look up, and said threateningly, as a few curious and puzzled-looking parishioners brushed past: 'You get it, shit face?'

Quite how the addressee could simultaneously be a cockhead and a shit face did not occur to the addresser but such crude speechmaking came to him naturally although it made his slightly better educated brother cringe.

But Simple Simon did not cringe; indeed Simple Simon never cringed. 'I get it, Limpy,' he said calmly but thickly and dully, without expression.

'And if you stuff up?'

'I won't, so back off, eh,' said an unperturbed Simple Simon.

Eric the Limp was noted for his aggressive and threatening disposition but Simple Simon was not easily intimidated by such a young, thin, sickly-looking, acne-faced petty crook and was perfectly capable of meeting aggression with aggression.

'Now you know exactly what to do don't you,' said Tatts McIndoe – slowly – who didn't himself know what Simple Simon was expected to do for his total of five thousand dollars but pretended he did.

'Yes,' said Simple Simon slowly and without expression. 'Big Ben told me the other day when I visited him in The Lake. And he told me not to say nothing to yous. Now I'm going into Mass if that's okay with you, Tatts? Limpy? It is Our Lord's birthday you know.'

'We know, Simon,' said Tatts McIndoe kindly. 'Merry Christmas, mate.'

'What does he bloody-well have to do for Big Ben to get five farting grand?' asked Eric the Limp of his brother when Simple Simon was gone into the church carrying his Countdown bag of money.

'I really don't know,' said Tatts McIndoe. 'Drugs maybe?'

'Farting Jesus, it must be a big deal,' said Eric the Limp.

He was right of course. It was a very big deal indeed.

Chapter 2

Angela Ravensthorpe arrived in Wellington late that same Christmas day more than thirty hours after her sudden and urgent departure from England.

On a dreadfully chilly morning two days previous she had found herself in the over-heated office of the chief constable of the Merseyside police — to whom she had been compelled to surrender her warrant card, her radio, her phone and her own cell phone, her watch, even her wallet and its entire contents — being debriefed by a number of important-looking people whom she didn't know including three senior police officers (only one of whom was in uniform) and some mysterious men from the Home Office who had evidently trained up especially from London. Her own commanding officer from the drug squad was there as well as an observing representative from the federation, an older woman from police welfare, and of course the chief constable himself who sat behind his desk, rolling a biro between his thumb and first two fingers, saying nothing. She listened carefully, obediently, to what she was told, sat down nervously and carefully on the edge of a hard chair in the corner of the spacious office and read all the papers and documents she was given, stood up and went to the chief constable's desk to sign two of them where she was shown, as she was instructed to do, while the others in the room watched and waited silently; when she was finished she slipped her copies of the papers into the thin black valise from which she had taken them and looked up questioningly, nervously, at the woman from police welfare. That woman then led her to another room – taking the valise of documents with her – where she was required to remove her clothes (rather flashy, gaudy and cheap-looking by design) including her tights, underwear and shoes, and change into the clothes she was given which were in an especially and consistently cheap and casual style – worn, faded and somewhat frayed jeans, a black polo-neck sweater, a black scarf and a wine-coloured puffer jacket – from which she saw that all labels and brand identifications had been removed. For her feet she was given a pair of new white ankle socks and a shabby pair of white Nikes. Finally she was handed a cheap wrist-watch.

'But what about–' she wanted to ask: –my flat, all my clothes, my makeup, my Kindle and CDs, my furniture, all my belongings, Katsue my cat, everything? My whole life is back there. And my phone? I need my phone. And they've got all my money and my cash card and everything. Instead she said meekly: 'I was told that everything would be–'

'Everything's been taken care of, dear,' said the older woman sympathetically. 'Exactly as planned. As you were told. You'll see. So don't worry. But you must hurry now. There's no time to lose.'

She wasn't returned to the chief constable's office and she never again saw nor heard from him or any of the other men. She and the police welfare woman left by the garage exit where an unmarked car was waiting, blowing fumes into the frigid air. They were then driven by the federation rep to John Lennon Airport where he unloaded a somewhat battered suitcase on wheels and handed her a large black handbag.

'Good luck, Ange,' he said quietly, grimly, before returning to the idling car.

'Good luck, dear,' said the older woman, kindly and gently, as they shook hands. It was freezing cold outside the terminal but Angela noticed and remembered how warm and soft the other woman's hand was. 'Remember,' said the welfare woman before she returned to the car, within the warmth of which the driver was waiting, 'tickets, passport, a wallet, money, all in the handbag, everything else in the valise. Don't let them out of your sight.'

And then before she knew it – hot, tired to the point of exhaustion, stiff and somewhat confused, aching to use the toilet, have a shower, wash her hair, brush her teeth, and change into fresh clothes which she assumed were in the suitcase – she was turning in her new passport to a young and friendly New Zealand immigration officer at Auckland airport.

'Welcome home, miss,' he said.

Home? Of course. A New Zealand passport. Home.

Where did those, what, nearly thirty hours go? she wondered. Was I *really* in Hong Kong last night? Hong Kong. All that time flying. She was amazed, astonished, shocked, but, it must be admitted, and she admitted it to herself, hugely relieved. And then, somehow, another short flight and she was in the terminal at Wellington airport on an unbearably hot and sunny Christmas day – Christmas in the summer seemed so strange and foreign to her – where she was met by a man and a woman who didn't give their names, didn't speak, who took her to a flat somewhere on the fringes of the city.

'We'll be in touch,' said the man as he unloaded the suitcase from the car and handed her the keys to the flat.

Once inside the small flat, and without even looking around, she stripped to her underwear, lay on the soft bed, and fell into a dreamless sleep, unaware of her surroundings, unaware that it was Christmas day, a hot, sunny Christmas day afternoon at the end of the world. She awoke when it was almost dark, which was precisely when she should be waking up on Christmas morning at home in Liverpool, having no idea at first quite where she was.

And so, from the excitement and danger of the Liverpool underworld, this former member of the Merseyside police drug squad was left to her own devices in Wellington for the next few days. What a sudden change it was: for almost eight years she had worked undercover, day and night, successfully infiltrating the Liverpool underworld and helping in the identification, arrest and prosecution of three of that city's most notorious gangland leaders. Now she had nothing to do in a small, quiet antipodean city in the middle of the summer holidays; a place she didn't know; a place where no one knew her and she knew no one.

Part of her undercover success in Liverpool – in fact the principal contributor to her success – was that she was an orphan with no known relatives; this was quickly identified by the Merseyside police as making her ideal for undercover work for which early in her career she had been taken aside and trained. But finally, eventually – inevitably some said – when her identity became known to the Liverpool criminal class and her life was at risk the Merseyside chief constable arranged her new identity, a new name and everything that went with it including a New Zealand passport, and sent her as far away from England as it was possible to go.

After a few idle days of rest – which, she admitted to herself, she needed to collect her thoughts and gather her strength – she was taken to the Wellington Central police station in

Victoria Street where she was to assume a new life and a new job as a humble uniformed woman police constable.

But her transition to the relatively simple and quiet life of a New Zealand WPC was quickly and rudely interrupted.

Meanwhile, early in the new year, the Merseyside police determined that Angela Ravensthorpe was no longer being sought by the Liverpool underworld; it seemed that the world of crime had in fact lost interest in her and her whereabouts when its citizens learned that she had fled to New Zealand where she had been brutally murdered.

Angela Ravensthorpe was never heard from again.

Chapter 3

Just after dawn on the first day of the next year the low summer sun, casting long very-early-morning shadows across Wellington, was almost as bright and hot as at noon-time. Two bored uniformed police constables – their caps pulled well down to shade their eyes from the low sun – stood more at ease than attention in the empty street at the opening of a nameless downtown alley now closed by police tape.

In the depth of that grimy and desolate canyon-like alley, where the air was warm and moistly humid despite the deep shade, a somewhat hung-over Detective Inspector Tim Glante stood looking glumly at the grey and lifeless-looking body of a young woman slumped back awkwardly against the alley wall of roughly pointed brick. She looked like a street prostitute, like the others, but unlike the others there were no signs of addiction.

Having seen enough, more than enough, Glante turned away, looked down to the crudely graffitied brick-wall end of the blank alley – what the hell's the point of graffiti if you can't read it, you dumb-arses, he thought – and ran his open hand down over his mouth, under his unshaven chin and down his neck and around the inside neck of his white t-shirt. It was the same t-shirt he had worn at the new year's eve party, now somewhat grubby, and stained with the expensive *pinot noir* he knew so well; too well. And so he felt distinctly gritty, grimy, sweaty, odorous and unkempt, in need of a shower and a shave, and dreadfully dry-mouthed. And a shit, he thought. A shit would be good, he thought. But the early-morning call from Central meant that bowel release and relief, and the niceties of morning ablutions, had been necessarily abandoned. And he felt vaguely nauseous. Too much of the *pinot* as usual, he thought. He briefly envied Pansy, his wife, who hadn't drank much – surprisingly, or perhaps not given her heritage, she never did – and, having got up with him, to make him a cup of his favourite sweet black tea, was now almost certainly asleep again in their bed in their large and rambling Hataitai home.

He glanced again at the unmoving figure against the wall. He noted the torn low-cut top, the dull grey face, lips turned blue, and the typical red bruising around her lovely slender neck and under her chin. Amazing, he thought. Exactly the same as the others, he thought. Five others. All exactly the same.

He decided then that he was utterly sick of violence; sick of the sight of dead bodies; sick of the sick and twisted minds of so many criminals; sick of the slick over-educated barristers who belittled his work as they defended the indefensible. Altogether, after more than forty years as a policeman, the last twenty-five in CIB, he was utterly sick of his work. And now just when he thought he'd got the bastard – as he referred to him – he found he hadn't. He's slipped away, again, he thought. The bastard's slipped away.

His birthday later in the year would mark the beginning of his retirement and he was glad. Pansy too was glad. They were going to sell the Hataitai house and move to tranquil friendly Martinborough away from all the crime and everything else unpleasant in Wellington. Martinborough. He never could have afforded such a lovely house and all that land in such a beautiful part of the country but it had been left to them – to her – when Pansy's widowed father died. A bit of luck there for a change he thought at the time. Still did.

But that – retirement amidst the timeless and beautiful vineyards of Martinborough – was months away. This was the ugly here and now: a Wellington alley. Now, on this already-hot summer morning, in this nameless blind alley littered with newspapers, greasy and sticky flattened pizza boxes and their buzzing blowflies, cigarette butts and used condoms, and the odour of stale urine, he stepped even deeper into the shade, closer to the clever young scientist working alone on his hands and knees in the filth and grime and squalor that was the floor of this sunless place.

The young scientist automatically stretched out his coveralled-arm and a latex-gloved hand – without looking around or up – to stop Glante from going closer. Glante stopped and stooped wearily to talk to the young man.

'So you got the call, Hawxwell?' he asked.

'Yep,' said the younger man. 'On duty as planned.'

'On your own?' asked Glante.

The young and somewhat socially-awkward genius Hawxwell, dressed in a blue forensic coverall, now turned to look around and up at the bent detective, whom he had always liked and admired – because he had always given the younger man the respect he thought he deserved, and did – but who on this early morning, bending over so his white-bristled face sagged and bagged horribly, looked tired and old. The young scientist felt vaguely sorry for the weary-looking detective.

'I thought it was best,' he said, pushing up his spectacles on his nose. 'New year's day and that. Overtime. And the fewer who know about this right now the better.'

'Good. I agree,' said Glante. 'The world will know about it soon enough. Photographer?'

'Been and gone.'

'Did you supervise?'

'Watched him like a hawk.'

'Hawxwell, eh. And nothing iffy or butty? No nosey-crap questions?'

'Nope. I know him well. He was fine. Bored. Just wanted to get home to his kids. Going to the beach I think. Very routine.'

Evidently satisfied, Glante relaxed. But only a little. 'I've got the wagon on the way to get her out of here,' he said. 'He's pretty wide but he should be able to back in here alright. But he won't be able to block the rubber-neckers – not that there are any yet – or press. But there will be. They'll be able to see everything.'

'Press are there now,' said Hawxwell. 'Look.'

Glante looked up the alley; the two constables were now having to deal with a dozen or so people jostling with each other.

'It'll be okay,' said Hawxwell reassuringly. 'They won't see anything out of the ordinary. Just enough. I'll see to it.'

'By the book, eh. Strictly by the book.'

'By the book absolutely, Aunty,' said Hawxwell. 'For sure.'

Glante hated the rhyming nickname but it had been his since the old days at Trentham and it was too late – and too hard and not worth the bother – to object to it now.

'The press though,' he said. 'Look at them. They would've got something already with their big-cock lenses I bet. One's even got binoculars.'

'Will it be alright?' asked Hawxwell anxiously.

'Yeah. For sure,' said Glante. 'Awkward angle though. But whatever they get, a sight like that?' He looked again at the young woman propped up so awkwardly against the alley wall. 'Jesus Christ, let them have what they get – I don't care – but they won't print it. Or air it. It's disgusting.'

'So what'll they do? What'll *you* do?'

Glante turned back to the working Hawxwell. 'I'll get an identikit done later. They can have that,' he said. 'So, what have you got so far?'

'I'll be down here for ages yet,' said Hawxwell. 'The full monty. For the record, you know. By the book as you say.'

'But? Meanwhile? I've got my own interim to do.'

'Well there's the handbag. Wallet. A few dollars. Some change. Nothing much else. No driver's licence though. No phone. No cards or keys. But it's okay. I made sure.'

'Give us a look,' said Glante.

'Over there,' said Hawxwell, pointing to his own hard black box-like case on the ground behind him; a black leather handbag lay beside it.

Glante bent painfully, picked up the wide-mouthed handbag, opened it, rifled through the contents and drew out a mustard-coloured women's wallet. He dropped the handbag to the ground and straightened up slowly, elbows out, his free left hand pressing into his lower left side, under his grubby white t-shirt, in a futile attempt to ease the aches in his lower back. The young coveralled and latex-gloved scientist – tall, thin, lithe, short-haired, bespectacled and distinctly boyish – evidently comfortably at ease in this ghoulish setting, on the filthy alley floor, frowned with concern.

'You alright, Aunty?' he asked the older man.

'Headache, nausea, dry horrors, lumbago, sciatica, rheumatism, arthritis, gout in one knee, slipped disc, muscle spasms down the back, enlarged prostate, old age, cancer of the every-damn-thing probably. You name it, boy, and I've probably got it,' said Glante from his now erect and less painful position.

'You're kidding, right?' said the younger man. Hopefully.

Glante nodded patiently while opening the wallet. 'Kidding? Yeah. Fit as a fiddle,' he said with bitter sarcasm.

He looked up from his wallet inspection.

'No ID,' he said. 'No licence, no credit cards, no ATM card, no nothing. Twenty-five dollars only.'

'I know,' said Hawxwell. 'No phone either. Going to make it hard isn't it?'

Glante nodded thoughtfully. 'Hard alright,' he agreed. 'But the identikit.'

'So—' said Hawxwell hesitatingly, doubtfully. '—everything *is* okay isn't it?'

'Amazing,' said Glante brightly. 'Excellent. Thanks.' He dropped the wallet into the open black handbag.

'No witnesses I suppose?' asked Hawxwell kneeling up, resting back on his heels, a fine brush in one hand. He adjusted his spectacles again.

'I doubt it. New year's eve? But we'll check all the clubs around here,' said Glante. 'What do *you* think?'

Hawxwell shrugged. 'Doubt it,' he said.

'Here's hoping,' said Glante 'Don't need complications though. I'll need that report but. Quick as you can but every little detail. Crossed Is and dotted Ts and all that crap-shit. Can't be too careful. Upstairs and that. I'm treading on eggshells *and* thin ice with this one.'

'I know. Tomorrow afternoon latest,' said the young scientist. 'Don't worry.'

'I'm not. But it really does look like him doesn't it.' It wasn't a question.

'Definitely does. No one could doubt it. He's all over it.'

'The one-handed strangulation. The strength. The grip. The brutality,' said Glante, thoughtfully stroking his bristled chin. 'Amazing really.'

'I know,' said Hawxwell. 'Every detail. But,' he added, 'I better get on.'

'Yeah, me too,' said Glante wearily. 'But you take care of her when the wagon comes, eh. You know what to do.' He looked up to the street where the two constables at the alley's narrow entrance were having to deal with reporters, photographers and television cameras, their long lenses straining to get a view down the alley to the crime scene. 'Vultures waiting,' he added.

'Quick, eh,' said Hawxwell.

'Wonder why?' said Glante with a wink. 'Still, better get it over and done with.'

He waved to the small group still jostling at the head of the alley so early on that first day of the year. 'I'm coming, I'm coming,' he called. And then, to Hawxwell: 'I can see it now, mate. The Welly Alley Strangler strikes again. Fear stalks the capital's streets. Pretty young prostitute victim number six. Mayor questions police action. Etcetera-blah.'

'It'll blow all their theories out of the water, won't it,' said Hawxwell.

'Yeah. Well their theories are only the theories I gave them. I thought we had the bastard,' said Glante. 'Everyone thought we had him. But he's doing three in The Lake for bugger all.'

'I know,' said Hawxwell.

'Assaulted a bouncer at a strip joint. Tried to strangle him. Like this I suppose. But the bouncer was too good for him. Not like the girls.'

Hawxwell nodded. He was bored. He'd heard it all before from the frustrated old detective.

'We got him for that at least,' added Glante. 'Three in The Lake.'

'But now?'

Glante shrugged. 'I'll get the bastard. I'll get him,' he said. 'If it's the last thing I do.'

He stepped carefully across to the young woman against the wall and looked down at her unmoving form.

'Okay, girl,' he said quietly. 'I know where you're heading. I'll be seeing you later.' And then he turned away, back to the working scientist and said: 'I'm outa here, mate. I'll see you later.'

'Later, Aunty,' said Hawxwell. 'Oh, and by the way,' he added.

Glante waited.

'Happy new year,' said Hawxwell.

'Whoopee-shit-dee-do,' said a nauseous Glante as the smiling young scientist, so happy in his macabre work, returned smilingly to his hands-and-knees position beside the grey-faced, blue-lipped, bruised and crooked body on the alley floor. And so say all of us, added Glante to himself. Now, meet the press, Glante. Meet the bloody press but keep it low-key. Soon all the world, his mother and brother and mutt will know about name unknown, female, aged mid-thirties, evidently the sixth miserable victim of the notorious Welly Alley Strangler.

And as he began to move out of the scene, to trudge reluctantly back to the street and the impatiently waiting members of the press, he thought he heard – he definitely *did* hear – the unmistakable sound of gas escaping suddenly and violently from a human anus. Surely not? He looked back and down at Hawxwell, gave him a quizzical look, but Hawxwell, who was looking up at him, merely shook his head slowly and slightly in silent denial and shifted his eyes sideways and meaningfully to the female figure lying so crookedly against the alley wall. Both men grinned conspiratorially, irreverently, as they resumed their respective duties.

Meanwhile, of all the people affected or about to be affected by the grisly scene in that nameless downtown alley, and the chain of five identical murders which had preceded it in a serial fashion, only Big Ben Pye was awake at that early hour on that new year's day. All the others – including Simple Simon, Tatts McIndoe, Eric The Limp, Paul-Frank Ratanui and his wife Faith, Ponytail O'Gorman and the Widow Partridge – were asleep and thus blissfully unaware of the meeting just ending between the young forensic scientist Rembrandt Hawxwell and the grossly hung-over Detective Inspector Tim Glante of Wellington Central CIB.

Chapter 4

Perhaps it was the sight and sound of eleven naked men (some carrying a towel) – wet, soapy and shampooey – their genitals flopping about freely and immodestly, running shamelessly, in fear and panic, from the doorless shower block; perhaps it was sound of hot water gushing noisily into twelve empty shower cubicles; or the clouds of hot steam billowing softly and damply into the changing room and beyond. It may have been the sharp cries of a single person's pain echoing around and emanating from the now empty white-tiled shower block. Or it may have been simply a response to that much under-rated, under-valued and under-used sense number six. Whatever the reason it was enough to cause C and C prison officer Paul-Frank Ratanui to abandon his morning routine peregrination around the west wing of Te Whareherehere – his assigned precinct for the first week of the new year of which this was the Monday – to investigate.

'Jeez, Fay, knew something was wrong,' he said to his wife Faith who had run all the way home when the police called her at the bank in Bay Road where she worked. He'd been given a tranquilizer by Doctor Wilkins and driven home by the police but he was still nervous and shaken – trembling slightly – as he sat in the kitchen with Faith. 'Had a thingie, a gut feeling, you know. Found him in the blimmin shower room.'

'Who, sweetie?' asked Faith sympathetically. 'Who'd you find?'

'Ponytail. Just lying there. Stabbed. In the side. Bleeding. Squealing.'

'Oh,' said Faith, unimpressed. 'Who's Ponytail?'

'Ponytail,' said Paul-Frank somewhat impatiently as if Faith the bank-teller should have a mental catalogue of all the inmates of Te Whareherehere who were her husband's charges. 'Ponytail Patsy. Patsy O'Gorman. Ponytail Patsy O'Gorman.'

'But who *is* he? And what happened to him?'

'Name's Patsy O'Gorman. Call him Ponytail because of his blimmin ponytail, obviously, grey, although he's mostly bald on top. Ponytail at the back. Just this harmless little con-man, love. Jeez, Fay, he's over sixty, about as little as you, and he wouldn't hurt a blimmin flea if it bit him on the cock.'

'So what happened?'

'No one else there. They'd all buggered off, nuddy like I said. Didn't want to be involved did they. And there was Ponytail lying on his back on the floor, naked and hairy, with a stab wound in his side, down low, down here–' Paul-Frank pressed the fingers of his right hand into his right side below the ribs '–or was it the other side? No, that's right, the right side. Anyway, the blood was all running into the water and spreading all over the tiled floor. His wet towel was floating in the bloody water on the floor beside him. There was all this cloudy reddy-brown water everywhere on the white tiles. And the place was full of steam because all the hot showers were still running. They must have dragged him out of the shower and done it.'

'Who?'

'Don't know, love. That's the thing of it. No one knows. At least no one's blimmin saying. Doubt they ever will.'

'Doesn't he – the Ponytail man – doesn't he know who did it?'

'Reckons he doesn't but I reckon he does. Too scared to say probably.'

'Oh, Pauly,' said Faith again. 'Was he okay?'

'Left a blimmin dagger thing behind on the floor and it started floating away towards the drain. I had to get it.'

'It floated?'

'Made of a clear plastic ruler. Must have pinched it from the computer room or the library or something. Sharpened to a point. All jagged. Was floating in all the bloody red water.'

'But, Pauly. Stabbed. Was he alright?'

'No,' said Paul-Frank. 'Not really. Was squealing blimmin bobsie-die like a stuck pig, all dopey and confused. Must have banged his head on the concrete floor when he went down. Don't think that helped.'

'Oh dear,' said Faith.

She stood up, went around the kitchen table to her husband's side, and rested her arm on his shoulder. Standing up she was only as tall as he was sitting down. Indeed, Paul-Frank Ratanui was a truly big man. Not only was he very tall – taller than even the tallest of his colleagues, and they were all necessarily tall – but he was broad, without being fat, and heavily muscled in his limbs as well as his neck, shoulders, back and chest. And his head was inordinately large, shaved and shiny. But while he was big, immensely strong, physically impressive and intimidating, his natural nature was kind and gentle. Indeed he was a tender and loving husband – Faith called him her gentle giant – a generous and helpful friend, kind to animals, children and the aged, indeed to any person or thing disadvantaged, weak or otherwise vulnerable including old criminals assigned to his care for the duration of their sentences.

Faith, on the other hand, was the opposite of her husband in every way. While he was tall, strong, brown, hairless, and strikingly handsome, she was short, frail, transparently white, with thick and wavy brown hair, and – it must be said – physiognomically plain. And while Paul-Frank was kind and gentle, Faith, evidently so tiny and delicate with plain looks, was clever, independent, quick-witted, astute and assertive; a not ungenerous woman but certainly robustly healthy with a steely will and a complete intolerance of fools. Indeed, Paul-Frank – so peculiarly innocent and naïve despite his great size and strength and somewhat hazardous occupation – depended on her to provide the intellect and common street-wisdom which he knew he lacked. It was a perfect partnership ideally equipped – with both the physical and intellectual resources – to wrestle with whatever challenges and setbacks life presented.

But for the moment both husband and wife were preoccupied with the stabbing of Ponytail O'Gorman whilst in the custody and care of Prison Officer Paul-Frank Ratanui.

Paul-Frank looked around at his wife standing at his shoulder.

'Spewed all over him, love,' he said with an embarrassed look; then he turned away and looked at the floor. 'Me. There and then. All my puffed wheat. Vegemite toast. My coffee. Everything. All floating in the water. He was naked and bleeding and looking up at me pathetically, whining, begging for help, poor little bastard, and I had to go and spew all over him and in the water.'

'Oh, my big softie,' said Faith, stroking the big and shiny head of her gentle but traumatized man in his blue and black C and C uniform with the purple logo. 'And it tastes so horrible doesn't it,' she added.

Paul-Frank turned and looked at his wife again with a puzzled expression. 'What does?' he asked.

'Sick. Vomit. Chuck. It leaves a horrible taste. Can you still taste it?'

'Don't care about that,' said Paul-Frank dismissively. 'Care that I done it all over poor little Ponytail.'

'But who would do that to him?' asked Faith naively. 'I mean a stabbing? In prison? And why?'

Paul-Frank shrugged his broad and bulky shoulders. 'It's The Lake isn't it,' he said as if that explained everything. 'No one knows who did it and probably never will. They called in the cops but they won't find anything. Never do. Doubt they even blimmin care for that matter. That's what it's like there. You know that. Anyway Ponytail gets picked on all the time. Especially since Big Ben arrived. Him and his gang in there are ruthless bastards.'

'Who's Big Ben?'

'Big Ben Pye,' said Paul-Frank. 'A real evil bastard. In for assault last year. But he's got his own men in there and he's running the place already.'

'Why does he pick on your Ponytail person?'

'Ponytail? Cause he's a toady little greasy smart-arse,' said Paul-Frank. 'Can't help it but he asks for it if you ask me.'

'Oh, it's horrible,' said Faith.

'Big Ben can't stand him for some reason.'

'Poor thing,' said Faith. 'Can't you do anything, love?'

'I usually look out for him,' said Paul-Frank sadly. 'But today--'

'So how is he? You still haven't told me.'

'Don't know,' said Paul-Frank. 'He was okay when I left. Alive. Suppose he'll be in the infirmary by now. Getting looked after by Watson and Crick.'

'Who's Watson and Crick?' asked Faith.

'Nurses in the infirmary. Crick's alright – nice – but Watson's a bit of a bitch.'

'Will they look after him?'

'Crick will. But he'll probably have to go to hospital,' said Paul-Frank. He turned in his chair. 'Come here, girl,' he said.

Faith turned and sat on his lap as if she were a little girl.

'Just a harmless little bloke, love,' he said.

'Not one of your violent crims?'

'Nah. Not a bit of it. Cunning but. Greasy and real cunning. Born liar.'

'How come?' Faith was intrigued by the sound of this Ponytail person.

'Runt of the litter I suppose,' said Paul-Frank. 'Ngati Porou I think. Ran away from home. Missed school. Lived rough. Moved to Wellington don't know when. Handsome but. Then, anyway. Turned to conning old ladies. Swindled some of them out of a few thousand dollars they could easily afford. Doing it for years.'

But Faith was still fascinated by Ponytail's name. 'But an East Coast Maori called, what did you say his real name was again?'

'Patsy O'Gorman?'

'Patsy O'Gorman. Really?

'Patrick I suppose,' said Paul-Frank. 'Don't know. Everyone just calls him Ponytail. He's always been just Ponytail.'

'Weird,' said Faith. 'It's a weird place you work.'

'Telling me? Anyway, most people think Ponytail's okay. Like him alright. Except Big Ben of course. Even his ladies, you know. One of them, his last victim – the Widow Partridge – visits him every blimmin week. Twice sometimes. She's an official.'

'Really?'

'Yeah. He reckons she wants to marry him when he gets out.'

'But he's a crook, Pauly. How could she? She's only his official.'

'It's bullshit,' said Paul-Frank. 'But that's what he's like. Full of it. Overflowing all over the place. Anyway, whatever, she won't like it when she hears about this.'

'She must be very strange woman,' said Faith. 'How old is she?'

Paul-Frank shrugged. 'Don't know really,' he said. 'Sixty-ish? About the same as him I suppose. Bit older maybe? Don't know exactly. Pretty rich. Visits The Lake for a hobby I think.'

Faith shook her head in wonderment at the strange people her husband had to mix with at work.

'Nice enough bloke, Fay, is Ponytail,' said Paul-Frank. 'Had a tough life. Done his time now. Only has a few weeks to go. Getting old. And the Widow Partridge will make sure he goes straight. That's what he says anyway.'

Faith was still on his lap so Paul-Frank laid his heavy head on her breast.

'Oh Jeez, Fay,' he said suddenly, lifting his head and looking at Faith in despair. 'He's only got a few weeks to go and he got stabbed in my wing, on my watch, and then I had to blimmin spew all over him.'

'Oh, Pauly,' said Faith sympathetically. 'You've got to get out of there.'

'Know,' said Paul-Frank giving Faith an affectionate squeeze.

'Ouch, Pauly,' she winced. 'You forget your own strength.'

'Sorry, love,' said Paul-Frank 'Anyway, hate that job now. Better get out as soon as I blimmin can, eh.'

'I think you should,' said Faith.

And so he did.

Chapter 5

The human resources committee of judges and magistrates of the Department of Courts and Corrections, Wellington, was sympathetic to Prison Officer Paul-Frank Ratanui's request for a transfer. Indeed, the committee members – especially the principal judge of the number one permanent criminal court, The Honourable Justice Dame Alexis Prohm, OBE, and the other lady justices of the first and second permanent criminal courts – rather liked the idea of such a big, strong and handsome young fellow working for them, protecting them from the potentially rampantly maniacal criminals they had to deal with every working day. And so a transfer to the court security division was approved and Paul-Frank was appointed to portal and prisoner duty at the number one permanent criminal court on the Court Road. It was there he reported for duty having served a statutory fortnight's notice at Te Whareherehere where, on his last day, he turned in his baton and helmet – no weapon or protective headwear was required at his new post – and exchanged his steel-capped boots for uniform shoes, of a size so big they had to be especially imported from Germany, that were light, pliable, supportive and especially comfortable.

'How's Ponytail, nurse?' he asked Nurse Watson at his farewell afternoon-tea shout. He was holding a chunky standard-issue C and C tea cup in his large hand.

'If you mean Mr O'Gorman,' said the small, neat, fussy and unpleasant Nurse Watson who was heavily burdened with a large superiority complex, 'he was transferred to hospital. Late last night as a matter of fact.'

'Oh, god,' said Paul-Frank. 'Why?'

'Nothing too bad if it's any of your business which it's not as you're leaving us,' said the nurse. 'But he needed hospital care. And he was delirious.'

'Delirious?' asked a puzzled Paul-Frank. 'What does that mean?'

'It means he was hallucinating,' said Nurse Watson condescendingly. 'Confused and rambling like the silly little crooked idiot he is at the best of times.'

'Don't mean what does delirious mean,' said an annoyed Paul-Frank; he had never liked Nurse Watson. 'I mean what does it mean about his condition? His health and welfare?'

'Could be the medication he's on. Fever. Fighting infection. I'm not sure. But it's definitely not good news, Mr Ratanui,' said Nurse Watson with a cruel smile. 'I must say, not good news at all.'

'Is he going to die?'

'Yes.'

'Oh god, no,' said Paul-Frank despairingly .

'Eventually,' added the nurse patronizingly. 'As we all must. That is our destiny. But not yet. I don't think so. Doctor Wilkins doesn't think so either.'

'Oh, thank god,' said a relieved Paul-Frank.

'But you never know,' added Nurse Watson quickly, with a slow shake of her knowing medical head. 'You never know when it comes to stabbings and haemorrhaging and fever and funny little old and unhealthy Maori men like scruffy Mr O'Gorman. No offence mind.'

'Oh, god,' said Paul-Frank again. 'Does the Widow Partridge know what happened? About this? About him going to hospital?'

'*Mrs* Partridge – a very respectable lady I must say – was there with him last night,' said Nurse Watson. 'I didn't approve of course but doctor said it was alright. She is after all his official visitor. And she was very grateful.'

'Did he know she was there? Was he *compos mentis* enough?'

'The patient was alert enough under the circumstances,' said Nurse Watson. 'Mrs Partridge was at his bedside all the time if you must know. Even as Doctor Wilkins made the decision to transfer him to hospital.'

'Oh, my god,' said Paul-Frank yet again. He tipped back his large head to drain the tea cup before adding: 'Poor old Ponytail.'

'The good lady even went with Mr O'Gorman in the ambulance,' said Nurse Watson. 'I didn't agree with it but Doctor—'

'Hope he's alright,' interrupted Paul-Frank. 'He's really pretty harmless you know.'

Nurse Watson shook her head slowly. 'He's a criminal, Mr Ratanui,' she said. 'A hardened criminal. Always was. Always will be. It's in his DNA.'

Later Paul-Frank was taken aside by Nurse Crick, a much kinder nurse than her colleague; her kindness showed in her face where all inner traits, good and bad, eventually find expression.

'Don't worry about Ponytail,' she said quietly. 'Watson's just trying to scare you.'

'So what do *you* think,' asked Paul-Frank.

'Frankly, Mr Ratanui, to tell you the truth, I personally think Ponytail was putting it all on to get out of here and into hospital.'

'What? Why?'

'I really don't know,' said Nurse Crick mysteriously. 'Can you think of a reason?'

'No. Of course not,' said Paul-Frank. 'Unless it's to get away from whoever stabbed him. That could be it. Big Ben maybe. So you think he'll be okay?'

'The stab wound really wasn't that bad you know,' said the kindly nurse with a knowing and reassuring smile. 'Superficial really. A lot of drama for nothing. Worthy of an Oscar if you know what I mean. I think he'll be fine. Really. Just fine.'

'Nice old bloke you know,' said Paul-Frank. 'Pretty harmless really.'

'I know,' said Nurse Crick gently. 'I know.'

Chapter 6

The first week of Paul-Frank Ratanui's court career passed quickly and uneventfully; quickly because everything was new and there was so much to learn and understand; especially uneventfully compared with any given week at the event-filled Te Whareherehere where he would have experienced more stress-inducing tension and unrest in half-an-hour than he had experienced in a full week of routine duty at the number one permanent criminal court.

'What a week, Max,' he said to Max Bridlington, his white-haired senior partner in the court. 'Tried to understand what was going on, eh, but Jeez, today, never understood a blimmin thing.'

It was late on Friday afternoon – the last day of that first week – and Paul-Frank and his partner were sharing a jug of cold beer in the warm garden bar of *The Scales of Justice*. And although Paul-Frank was enjoying both the beer and the company his bulk didn't properly fit into the small, narrow and terribly-fashionable garden furniture chair which seemed to be *de rigueur*. As there was no choice he had to perch awkwardly on the chair's edge while Max, who was long but not nearly as broad, was able to sit back comfortably for the duration.

'Fraud and financial trials, business and corporate affairs, they're always like that,' said the experienced Max who had been working at the court for fifteen years before which, like Paul-Frank, he had been a prison officer at Te Whareherehere. 'I don't understand them either so you're not alone, mate. Tenny-rate they don't come along very often.'

'Good,' said Paul-Frank. 'Don't like mysteries.'

'Interestingly,' said Max, leaning forward over the small but *très à la mode* table that stood between them and upon which stood their jug of beer and their glasses, 'if we can't understand what's going on, what they're all talking about, then neither can the jury. Which is the point. It means one of the barristers is trying to confuse them.'

'They do that?'

'Of course they do,' said Max leaning back in his chair. 'The judge will often pull them up, especially if the other chap objects. Or lady chap. There's lady barristers now all over the place. Lady judges too as you can see this week. Anyway, you must have seen her do that this week.'

'Do what?'

'Tell off the defence barrister for trying to confuse the jury.'

'Did,' said Paul-Frank. 'Know what you mean.'

'But they'll try it if they can,' added Max.

'Wow,' said Paul-Frank. 'So much to learn.'

'Believe me, my friend, barristers — any barrister — if they want, can explain things so simply that a monkey could understand. But if they want they can make you believe that black is white, up is down, bad is good, stripes are dots, that a mouse is an elephant and the moon's a balloon.'

'So they're liars?'

'Absolute liars sometimes,' said Max. He shared the remaining beer between their glasses and stood up with the empty jug. 'Tenny-rate, I'll get another jug.'

Paul-Frank was glad Max had offered. He wasn't sure he could easily get his broad behind out of his narrow chair and if he did that he could squeeze it back in again. When Max returned he topped up their glasses casually, sat down easily.

'Murders are the most understandable, Pauly,' he continued as if he'd never been away. 'Horrible as they are you can usually understand what's going on. Simple evidence.'

'Really?' Paul-Frank was intrigued.

They both drank their beer. Paul-Frank was enjoying this conversation and was pleased — flattered — that the older and wiser man was evidently enjoying his company.

'Oh, yes,' said Max. 'I've learned a lot about murder and murderers over the years.'

'Like what?'

'I reckon that there's only three kinds of murderers.'

'Really?'

'Oh, yes,' said Max again. 'There's the nice, intelligent, well-educated middle-class and up murderers, men *and* women, it doesn't matter — real rich sometimes — who basically are happy to serve time as the price for getting rid of someone they hate, usually an unfaithful spouse. The eternal triangle you know.'

Paul-Frank was fascinated which encouraged Max to continue.

'They do little if anything to hide their crime and often hand themselves in. If they don't they soon get caught anyway and when they do, and in court, they only put up a flimsy defence. Or no defence. I've seen it many times. Those kind have no criminal history and will *never* offend again. You must have known them in The Lake? Model prisoners they are.'

Paul-Frank nodded. He knew the type well. But he said nothing; he was listening carefully.

Max took a long draught of his beer and so Paul-Frank followed.

'Then there are the violent misfits,' continued Max, wiping his mouth with the back of his hand. 'Career criminals. Real baddies. Dumb losers. Usually men. Low IQ. For some reason they think they're clever but they're basically stupid and so always get caught. They usually have a violent history and will always – *always* – offend again.'

'Know the type for sure,' said Paul-Frank. 'Wonder why *they* do it?'

'Usually it's revenge for some imagined slight or insult or something like that,' said Max. 'They're in a gang or something. Often it's drug related. Or territorial. Something anyone normal would consider trivial but it's important to them in their twisted view of the world.'

Paul-Frank grimaced. He *definitely* knew that type.

'Most of them are mad as hatters, you know,' said Max. 'Complete psychos. You've must have seen them in The Lake.'

'Know them well,' said Paul-Frank. 'Know the type. Never liked them. So touchy.'

They each took another drink.

'What about the third type?' asked Paul-Frank.

'Eh?'

'You said there were three kinds of murderers,' said Paul-Frank.

'Oh yeah. Well, they're rare. Specially in this country,' replied the older man. 'But there's one of them on the loose right now, right here in Wellington,' he added grimly.

'Eh?'

'The psychopathic serial killer, Pauly,' said Max.

'You mean the Welly Alley Strangler?'

'That's the one,' said Max. 'The Welly Alley Strangler. What a name, eh.'

'Do you know something about him?' asked Paul-Frank. 'The Welly Alley Strangler?'

'Not really,' said Max Bridlington. 'Nothing in particular. But he seems typical of the type.'

'Does he?'

'Oh, yes,' said Max. 'They plan their killings meticulously. Have a signature style but leave no tangible evidence. Take great pride in their cleverness, not getting caught. And they pay close attention to news stories about their deeds. It seems they love the idea of fooling the police.'

'Seems to have the blimmin police fooled for sure,' said Paul-Frank.

Max nodded thoughtfully. 'They thought they had him you know,' he said.

'Who? The police?'

'That's what I heard,' said Max. 'Rumour was that they had him locked up for something trivial and just needed the time to prove he really was the Strangler.'

'Wonder,' wondered Paul-Frank. 'Wonder if he was in The Lake. Might have known him without knowing it.'

'You very well might have,' said Max.

'But what happened?'

'Well, there was that new year's eve murder wasn't there,' said Max. 'That poor mysterious unidentified girl.'

'Been in all the papers and TV and everything,' said Paul-Frank. 'Faith said they don't know who she is.'

'No. No ID. Nothing at all,' said Max, 'Apparently there is an official photo of her face taken by the police but it's so horrible they decided not to release it. That's what I heard.'

Paul-Frank grimaced at the thought.

'They've released an Identikit drawing,' said Max. 'Been in the paper and on telly. No help apparently.'

Paul-Frank nodded. Faith had said the same thing.

'All the hallmarks of the Welly Alley Strangler though,' said Max. 'Which means he's still out there somewhere so they have to do a re-think. Start all over again.'

'Wonder who it is,' said Paul-Frank wonderingly.

'Rumour has it they *really* know who it is this time,' said Max who seemed to know what he was talking about. 'But they can't find him. He's disappeared.'

They both took the last of the beer and ruminated inwardly.

'But they'll get him eventually,' said Max at last.

'Reckon?'

'Most serial killers get caught eventually,' said Max. 'They start skiting about how clever they are. Let something slip. Somehow. To someone. Can't help it. Pride and that. Just a matter of time really.'

Paul-Frank nodded.

'I suppose Aunty knows that,' said Max. 'Just has to wait.'

'Who's Aunty?'

'He's the OC on the case,' said Max. 'Officer in charge. Grumpy old CIB bloke but he's alright. Been around forever. You'll see him in court one day. Or in the canteen. Comes in here sometimes too. Likes his beer but he's a wine drinker really.'

'Funny name,' said Paul-Frank.

'Nickname,' said Max. 'Detective Inspector Tim Glante. Aunty rhymes with Glante see.'

'What a job.'

'He's already got six poor girls on his hands,' said Max. 'Six. Imagine it.'

'Prozzies and addies,' said Paul-Frank. 'Faith read it in the paper.'

'Not the last one,' said Max. 'Not an addict. Prostitute probably they reckon.'

'Weird that no one recognizes her,' said Paul-Frank. 'Knows who she is. She must have had clients and that.'

'They probably wouldn't talk,' said Max.

'Wouldn't want to get involved I suppose,' said Paul-Frank.

'Sad, isn't it,' said Max. 'Doesn't matter what they were, no one deserves to die like that.'

'No,' said Paul-Frank, shaking his head slowly.

'Tenny-rate I'm sure we'll hear all about it in detail before long.'

'What do you mean?'

'Well, when he's caught – he *will* get caught – the trial will be in our court for sure,' said Max. 'Not looking forward to that given what I've heard already.'

'Like what?'

'Nothing official, Pauly,' said Max quietly. 'And it's not in the papers or anything. But they reckon he must be a big over-sized giant of a bloke – bit like you I suppose – who chooses small young women, holds them up against a wall by the neck with one hand, strangles them to death as they struggle, and then lets them fall to the ground.'

'Jesus Christ,' said a shocked Paul-Frank. He'd never heard such detail and Faith told him everything she read in the paper.

'And always at night down a dark alley.'

'Like the last one,' said Paul-Frank remembering.

'Disgusting, isn't it,' said Max. 'Who could do something like that?'

Paul-Frank shook his head again. 'Horrible,' he said.

They finished their beer. Paul-Frank felt vaguely troubled, uneasy, about what he had heard about the Welly Alley Strangler. He felt as though it had spoiled what had been an enjoyable first week. He decided it was time to go home to Faith.

'Better go, e hoa,' he said.

'Me too,' said Max. 'But I enjoyed the beer, my friend. And the talk. We'll do it again, eh. Next Friday night?'

'Yeah,' said Paul-Frank as he stood up; the small chair came with him and he had to reach back awkwardly to pry it free from his behind.

They stood together outside *The Scales of Justice* on the busy Court Road. It was a warm and beautiful evening.

'You lasted longer than me,' said Max.

'Where?'

'In The Lake,' said Max. 'What happened in the end?'

'Found an old con stabbed in the showers. Blood everywhere.'

'Was that unusual?'

'Unusual to be that bad. A stabbing,' said Paul-Frank. 'Harmless old joker too. Didn't deserve anything like that.'

'What was he in for?'

'Diddled some rich old biddies out of some money. Not much really,' said Paul-Frank.

'Sounds like you liked him.'

'Didn't *like* him exactly,' said Paul-Frank. 'But didn't mind him either. Little and old and blimmin harmless. Got picked on so I used to look out for him.'

'But you couldn't stop him from being knifed?'

'No. And he looked so awful lying naked on the floor with a blood oozing out of his side. Blood everywhere. Made me sick. Spewed all over him. Jeez, didn't like that, Max. That I spewed all over him.'

Max Bridlington shrugged as if to ask so what?

'Was the last straw, that's all. Last blimmin straw as far as I was concerned. So. Got a transfer. And here I am.'

'Tenny-rate, who did it?'

'What?'

'Stabbed your little mate? The one you vomited all over.'

'No idea,' said Paul-Frank. 'Police came in but they never found out. Not officially anyway.'

'What about the knife?'

'Sharpened plastic ruler.'

'Yeah? No dabs?'

'No. Only his from pulling it out,' said Paul-Frank although he had wondered about that. He thought the stabber must have held the plastic dagger with a towel because apart from the towels that some of them carried they were naked and certainly none was wearing gloves.

'No cameras?'

'Not in the showers,' said Paul-Frank. 'Caught everything going in and coming out but not in the shower block itself.'

'CCTV everywhere at court,' said Max. 'Everywhere these days. But none in The Lake when I was there. Not invented I don't think. They could get away with murder. Not literally but you know what I mean. What was his name again? Your little mate?'

'No mate exactly,' said Paul-Frank. 'His real name's Patrick O'Gorman – Patsy – but everyone calls him Ponytail. Ponytail O'Gorman. Cause of his–'

'Ponytail,' interrupted Max.

'Yeah,' said Paul-Frank. 'He got moved to hospital when I left but he'll be alright. Tough scrawny little bugger really. Could be back inside by now but he'll be out soon.'

'Back to his old tricks? Old cons can't stop.'

'Dunno,' said Paul-Frank with a slight shrug. 'There was one lady – one of his victims – he said she wanted to marry him. According to him anyway. So maybe–'

'I doubt it, my friend,' said Max. 'I don't know your mate but they don't you know. Turn over new leaves. My guess is you'll be seeing him in court or somewhere before long.'

'Hope not,' said Paul-Frank. And he meant it. 'He really is such a harmless and likable old bugger but I really don't want to see him again. Don't think I will. Hope I'm right.'

But as it turned out he couldn't have been wronger.

Chapter 7

'Where's the phone?'

The Widow Partridge was cowering on the floor where she had been pushed by the taller of the two intruders.

'We want the phone, lady,' said the tall young intruder Eric the Limp.

The lady in question looked up at her spotty assailant and his short partner with a mixture of scorn, contempt, low regard and only a little — almost no — fear. Even cowering on the thickly-carpeted floor of the large and expensively- and tastefully-furnished living room of her Oriental Bay penthouse apartment — with panoramic city and harbour views through a large picture window — she looked elegant, well-groomed and dignified. Her slight figure, in a blue floral skirt and a white twin-set set off with a double row of creamy glowing pearls, was supported awkwardly on one elbow, which was already red and sore from a carpet graze through her cardigan, while her other arm was held up to shield her smooth and still-lovely face which was framed by short hair cleverly and expensively arranged and tinted by Wellington's finest coiffeur. Her blue brocade slippers had come off and were lying crookedly near her stockinged feet. She was trembling a little, more from discomfort than fright, as the two juvenile thugs with whom we are already familiar — dressed even on this fine Sunday afternoon in their ill-fitting tight black trousers, black vinyl jackets, white open-neck shirts and black heeled boots, which she could see from her prone position were dirty and scuffed – stood over her threateningly. The taller of the two was gripping a short cosh in his right fist. It was secured to his wrist with a knotted leather thong and was usually concealed up the sleeve of his jacket; but he was using it now to threaten the brave widow.

'It's over there,' said the Widow Partridge calmly as she pointed to the cream desk-phone sitting on the china cabinet behind her.

'Not *that* phone, you stupid old cow,' said Eric the Limp with a wave of his cosh. '*The* cell phone. Ponytail's cell phone.'

Seeing the stubby weapon in the tall man's hand the Widow Partridge suddenly *was* frightened.

'Oh, please don't hurt me,' she begged. Despite her bravery, her determined defiance, she now began weeping a little; her eye make-up ran blackly and wetly down her pink and unwrinkled cheeks.

Despite her plea, or perhaps perversely because of it, Eric the Limp raised his cosh as if ready to strike and the Widow Partridge instinctively moved her shielding arm to take the blow and so protect her head.

'Stop it, Limpy!' shouted the short Tatts McIndoe.

'What?' shouted Eric the Limp angrily in reply; he held the cosh still in the air.

'Limpy,' said Tatts McIndoe calmly, 'who do you think you are addressing with your indignant what, you twat?'

'What?' said Eric the Limp again as he lowered his cosh-carrying hand.

'We do not strike harmless, helpless and refined old ladies,' said Tatts McIndoe. 'In fact we don't strike anyone. Now put that stupid thing away.'

At which command Eric the Limp slipped the cosh up the sleeve of his jacket.

Meanwhile Tatts McIndoe turned to the Widow Partridge and said: 'Do not concern yourself, madam, we shall not strike you. You have my word as a gentleman and a scholar.' And then turning again to Eric the Limp he said: 'And I don't give a horse's balls what Big Ben said.'

'You'll give your own balls if we don't get that phone,' said Eric the Limp.

'I am not concerned, my brother,' said Tatts McIndoe dismissively. 'Look at yonder lady. She favours our Nan somewhat. Indeed, she quite reminds me of our Nan.'

'Eh?' said Eric the Limp.

'Well, before the overdose anyway,' said Tatts McIndoe quickly. 'Now come along, dear madam,' he said directly, pleadingly, to the Widow Partridge. 'Just surrender the silly little phone and we'll leave you alone.'

'May I sit up? Please?' asked the lady whose temporary fear of violence had quickly evaporated in the face of the utter stupidity of the two young fools in black. Her contempt for them was now without measure.

'Yes, of course, go on, Nan,' said Tatts McIndoe. 'It is obvious to yours truly, namely me and I, that you are not entirely comfortable down there on the axminster. Top quality by the way. And a nice pattern. Tasteful. Sit up on the couch there, make yourself comfortable, and tell us about Ponytail's little phone.'

'Thank you, son,' said the Widow Partridge sincerely as she struggled awkwardly – and a little painfully, it must be said, due to her ageing hips – adjusting her dress and her cardigan, primping her hair, and eventually sitting primly on the edge of the couch. She extended one leg and used its dainty stockinged foot to draw the slippers across the carpet to her, one at a time, and bent to put them on, one at a time, slowly and a little painfully.

'Come on, lady,' said Eric the Limp impatiently, swinging his cosh again idly. 'Stop farting about. Just give us the phone.'

'Limpy,' said Tatts McIndoe. 'Please!'

'What?'

'Your language. In front of Nan. And put that thing away.'

'She's not our Nan,' said Eric the Limp as he tucked the cosh up into his sleeve again. And then of the Widow Partridge he asked again, roughly: 'So where's Ponytail's cell phone, lady? We know he gave it to you.'

'How do you know?' asked the Widow Partridge.

'We *know* stuff,' said Eric the Limp smugly.

More comfortable now, her slippers on, sitting straight-backed on the edge of the couch, the Widow Partridge drew a lacy handkerchief from the sleeve of her white cardigan and began wiping her moist face, wiping away the smudged mascara, before finding a clean spot and gently, daintily, wiping her nose. That all done, she returned the screwed-up handkerchief to its home, rested her hands together on her lap, and looked up, outwardly innocent but inwardly defiant, at the two intruders whom she now considered no better than naughty children.

'There's *my* cell phone,' she said.

'But where's Ponytail's phone? The one he gave you in the infirmary,' said Eric the Limp. 'We know he did.'

'I don't know,' said the Widow Partridge.

'What do you mean you don't know?'

'I mean I don't know,' said the Widow Partridge defiantly. 'I really and truly don't know.'

'Tell us more, lady.'

'I posted it,' said the Widow Partridge.

'Meaning?'

'Meaning I took it to the post office, put it in one of those bubbly bag things, and posted it.'

'Farting Jesus,' said Eric the Limp in frustration.

'Shut up, Limpy,' said Tatts McIndoe sharply. And turning to the Widow Partridge he asked, softly and gently: 'Who did you post it to, dear lady?'

'I don't know.'

'Why don't you know?' asked Tatts McIndoe patiently. 'Don't you remember or what?'

'She's lost her marbles,' said Eric the Limp. 'That's why.'

'I most definitely have *not* lost anything of the sort,' said the Widow Partridge angrily to Eric the Limp. And then, turning to Tatts McIndoe, she said calmly: 'You see, son, poor dear Ponytail gave me the address on a tissue. I just copied it onto the bubble bag and threw away the tissue. It meant nothing to me and I simply don't remember what it was.'

'It's bullshit!' shouted Eric the Limp angrily. 'A steaming heap of fresh, warm and wet bullshit. I can tell.'

'Limpy,' said Tatts McIndoe scoldingly. 'Shut your hole.'

He returned his attention to the Widow Partridge.

'Very well,' he said quietly and calmly. 'One thing at a time. Now, madam, let's start with *your* phone. Your cell phone.'

'Yes?'

'Well, where is it?'

'It's in my handbag,' said the Widow Partridge. 'Over there.'

Tatts McIndoe went to the Steinway at the end of the room in front of the large picture window with panoramic views across the city and up the beautiful dark-blue harbour whitely dotted with Sunday afternoon yachts.

'Nice view by the way,' he said. 'Yachts.'

The Widow Partridge's handbag lay on the closed top of the piano beside a large hand-coloured wedding photo obviously taken in times past. Tatts McIndoe picked up the framed picture. 'Your wedding?' he asked.

The Widow Partridge nodded. 'My Pete,' she said.

'Nice,' said Tatts McIndoe.

He carefully put back the framed photo on the polished black lid of the piano and began rifling quickly through the widow's handbag. He soon found her phone but couldn't open it without the code. He took it across the room to its owner and stood over her.

'Open it please, Nan,' he asked politely. 'If you will.'

The Widow Partridge looked quizzically at Tatts McIndoe for a moment, took the phone from him, opened it and returned it to his waiting hand. He swiped his way quickly through its files as its owner looked up and watched anxiously from her seated position on the couch. It didn't take more than a few seconds but the watching Widow Partridge could tell that the small young crook didn't like what he found in her phone; or, rather, he didn't like what he didn't find in her phone.

He looked from it down to her, sitting passively on the couch.

'No recordings?' he asked.

She, sitting quietly, impassively, her hands in her lap, looked up at her questioner with a puzzled expression.

'What?'

'Recordings. Sound files. On your phone.'

The Widow Partridge appeared genuinely baffled by the question.

'I don't know anything about sound files or recordings or anything of the jolly sort,' she said. 'Believe it or not I use it for a phone and sometimes to take photos. I know how to take photos.'

'We know all about you taking photos,' said Tatts McIndoe.

'Don't believe the old bitch,' said Eric the Limp.

Tatts McIndoe turned to Eric the Limp. 'Why should we not believe her?' he snapped. 'You don't know how to use your own phone. Why should she? She's old.'

'Not that old,' interjected the Widow Partridge.

'That's different,' said Eric the Limp.

'Well I believe her,' said Tatts McIndoe. 'There's nothing here.'

'Check the photos,' said Eric the Limp.

'Exactly what I was about to do, brother of mine,' said Tatts McIndoe.

He scrolled through the gallery of photos as the quietly defiant widow looked on.

'Here it is,' he said to his brother at last.

The Widow Partridge tensed but the brothers, standing together, looking down at the phone, didn't notice.

'That's the one,' said Tatts McIndoe. 'The new year's eve one that Ponytail had. She sent it to him alright.'

'But how come?' asked Eric the Limp peering closely at the little picture of two smiling figures, each holding a glass of red wine, standing in front of a "Happy New Year" banner which was stretched across a dark veranda decked out with bunting and coloured lights.

Tatts McIndoe looked down at the seated widow. 'How come you know Simple Simon?' he asked.

'I used to be his official,' said the widow. 'When he was in The Lake.'

'That's right,' said Tatts McIndoe remembering. 'I remember. So you still see him?'

'Sometimes I do,' replied the lady. 'I'm Ponytail's official too.'

'We know all about *that*,' said Tatts McIndoe. 'And we know *everything* about your Simple Simon too, don't you worry.'

He turned the phone to the Widow Partridge to show her the photo. 'So where was this taken?' he asked.

She couldn't see the picture at that distance but she didn't have to; she knew it well enough. 'At a new year's eve party,' she said.

'Where?' asked Tatts McIndoe. 'Whereabouts exactly.'

'In Martinborough,' said the Widow Partridge. 'The big hotel in Martinborough.'

'He's with her? On new year's eve? In Martinborough?' queried Eric the Limp. 'Where the fart is Martinborough?'

'It's a posh town in the Wairarapa,' said Tatts McIndoe. 'Noted, I believe, for its *Pinot noir.*'

'Pee-noh what?'

'*Noir*,' said Tatts McIndoe condescendingly.

'How do you know this shit?' asked Eric the Limp.

'I read,' said Tatts McIndoe to his brother. And then, turning to the Widow Partridge, he asked: 'So who took the photo?'

'Oh, someone at the party,' said the Widow Partridge casually. 'A friend of Simon's I think.'

'So, Big Ben was correct in his conjecture,' said Tatts McIndoe to his brother.

'Eh?'

'Simple Simon was obviously not in Wellington on new year's eve,' said Tatts McIndoe. 'Clearly he was at this new year's eve party in Martinborough with this lady and some friends.'

'So?'

'So, he couldn't have done it,' said Tatts McIndoe.

'Done what?'

'Whatever Big Ben had paid him to do, you idiot. Remember?'

'He could've driven back to Wellington after the party,' said Eric the Limp.

'He can't drive,' said Tatts McIndoe. 'Couldn't get his licence. Too dumb. And he hasn't got a car anyway. I know that for a fact. So he did *not* do it. He could not do it. Big Ben was right. He clearly did not fulfil his side of the contract whatever it was.'

'What an arse fart,' said Eric the Limp. 'He got the dough and he never done it whatever it was. I wouldn't want to be him now. What are you doing?'

'I'm sending the photo to *my* phone,' said Tatts McIndoe. 'To show Big Ben again. Then I'm going to delete it. Sorry about that,' he added, looking up, addressing the Widow Partridge.

'He's seen it already when Ponytail showed him,' said Eric the Limp. 'That's how this all started.'

'He'll want to see it again,' said Tatts McIndoe.

'Wouldn't want to be Simple Simon,' said Eric the Limp with a shake of his head.

Chapter 8

Tatts McIndoe finished the send, deleted the photo from the Widow Partridge's phone, and handed it back to its owner who was waiting and observing them from her seated position on the couch.

'Thank you, Nan,' he said.

The Widow Partridge quickly checked the phone before holding it tightly in her lap.

'Listen, lady,' said Eric the Limp, leaning down towards her threateningly, 'we really want Ponytail's phone. So if you know what's good for you, and for him, the little dick, then you'll start telling the truth about where it is. Do you get it?'

'Do not speak to the dear lady like that,' said Tatts McIndoe.

'Shut your cake hole, Tatts,' said Eric the Limp without taking his eyes off the Widow Partridge. 'Now, lady, do you under-bloody-stand?'

'Of course I do,' said the Widow Partridge. 'I'm not stupid you know. But I *did* tell you the truth.' And then, out of the blue as it were, she asked: 'Did you smash in my door?'

'What?' Eric the Limp was distracted by the question.

'My door,' the old lady repeated. 'I take it you came up in my private lift – I don't know how you managed that – and the noise I heard when you arrived tells me you smashed in my door. Did you? Smash in my door?'

'Yeah, of course we bloody smashed in your stupid bloody door,' said an impatient Eric the Limp.

'But my lift?'

'My brother knows stuff like that,' said Eric the Limp. 'Piece of bloody cake to him.'

'So he, your brother here, whom you call Tatts, can skilfully hijack my private lift, bring it up ten floors, but can't open a common door lock?'

'We never had a bloody key to the door did we, you stupid old whore,' said Eric the Limp.

'Limpy. Please. Refrain from such crudenesses,' said Tatts McIndoe. 'Not only that and furthermore, if I have told you once I have told you a hundred times, sarcasm is the lowest form of wit?'

'Shut your hole again,' said Eric the Limp.

'Understand, dear lady,' said Tatts McIndoe slowly, ignoring his brother, his pride somewhat dented by the slur the widow had cast on his competence in the dark art of breaking and entering, 'of course I could have opened your oh-so-simple residential slash domestic Yale lock – I have of course opened many many locks of greater complexity in my time – but time, as they say, was of the essence if you will.'

'What the fart does that mean?' said Eric the Limp.

'He means you were in a hurry, Limpy,' said the Widow Partridge to Eric the Limp.

'How do you know my name?' said a shocked Eric the Limp at which the Widow Partridge merely smiled condescendingly. And then, turning to Tatts McIndoe, she said: 'So, Tatts, I suppose there'll be glass on the floor? All over the tiles?'

'His name too,' said a surprised Eric the Limp.

'I'm sorry about that,' said Tatts McIndoe. 'I really am.'

'Oh dear. Broken bloody glass,' said Eric the Limp sarcastically. 'Now, Ponytail's phone, you stupid old crone.'

'Hey!' said Tatts McIndoe. 'Don't speak to our Nan like that.'

'For fart's sake, Tatts, she's *not* our Nan.'

'You may be right, technically' said Tatts McIndoe, 'but she favours Nan and she deserves our respect.'

'Respect? She's Ponytail's old root.'

The Widow Partridge appeared unaffected by Eric the Limp's vulgarity but his brother was visibly shocked.

'What a dreadful thing to say about someone who reminds me of Nan,' he said with a shiver.

But Eric the Limp merely shook his head in frustration. 'Well she's not Nan so shut up,' he said to his brother before turning back to the Widow Partridge. 'Now, lady,' he continued, 'you smuggled a phone into The Lake – and that's illegal for a start which makes you a criminal – and you gave it to Ponytail and he got stabbed in the guts because of it and went to hospital and we know he gave the phone back to you when he was in the infirmary and we want it. Now. Get it, you cunning old bitch?'

'Uh uh,' said Tatts McIndoe to his brother by way of admonishment. 'She might be old and she might be cunning but don't call her that other word, Limpy. I don't like it.'

'What the fat fart?' said Eric the Limp in frustration before almost yelling the question: 'Come on. Who the fart did you post it to?'

'I'm sorry, young man,' said the Widow Partridge calmly, convinced now that where at first she had seen two dangerous young thugs she now saw a pair of stupid young mugs. 'I simply don't remember. You'll have to ask Ponytail himself. He's the one who gave me the address.'

'Yeah, right,' said Eric the Limp sarcastically. 'But the little shitbag's gone missing hasn't he.'

'What do you mean?' asked a suddenly alarmed Widow Partridge. 'I thought he was safe in hospital with his wound.'

'He's out of hospital, out of The Lake, free as a bird, on parole on compassionate grounds believe it or not,' said Tatts McIndoe contemptuously. 'You see, dear lady, we want him and his phone but we can't find either of them. Hence our visitation here today.'

'Oh dear,' said a worried Mrs Partridge. 'He was one of my cases.'

'One of your basket cases is right,' said Eric the Limp. 'One you're going to marry.'

'He's deluded about that poor chap,' said the Widow Partridge. 'But anyway he won't be one of my cases anymore.'

'Why not?'

'Obviously, brother of mine,' said Tatts McIndoe, 'Ponytail O'Gorman is no longer resident at The Lake. Thus Nan won't be visiting him there anymore.'

'And what about Simple Simon?' asked Eric the Limp.

'Yes, Nan,' said Tatts McIndoe, remembering. 'Where's Simple Simon? We can't find him either.'

'Oh, I really don't know about that.'

'But he was with you on new year's eve. At that party.'

'But we're not close friends or anything,' said the Widow Partridge. 'I haven't seen him since then. Isn't he at home?'

'We don't know where he lives,' said Tatts McIndoe. 'Do you?'

'No, I'm afraid I don't,' said the Widow Partridge. 'I don't really know him that well at all you know.'

'Then how come he was with you on new year's eve?' asked Eric the Limp angrily.

'I don't know,' said the Widow Partridge sharply. 'He was just there, that's all. There were lots of young people there.'

'I don't believe you, you old whore,' said Eric the Limp holding his cosh forward threateningly.

'Limpy,' interrupted Tatts McIndoe angrily. 'Please do not address Nan in that manner. And put that thing away.'

'She's not our Nan, you fart-head,' said Eric the Limp as he reluctantly returned the cosh to its place up the sleeve of his jacket. 'Anyhow, I *don't* believe her. The phone could be right here in this flat for all we know.'

The two young men were now uncertain what to do next. They looked at each other, their heads tilted queerly to one side, like puzzled monkeys trying to think; and then, giving up, they looked down again at the seated Mrs Partridge.

'Come on, Nan,' said Tatts McIndoe. It was a plaintiff pitiful plea utterly devoid of threat.

'She's not your bloody Nan,' insisted Eric the Limp. 'Now, lady, we – me and my brother – we don't believe you about nothing. We can't find Ponytail or his phone and we can't find Simple Simon but we *have* found you and so we're going to tear this place of yours apart to find that phone. We know what it looks like. We know the brand. We even know the number. So stand by to have your place totally trashed.'

'Hold the phone,' said Tatts McIndoe. 'No pun intended, Limpy, but I did not know we knew the number.'

'I know the farting number.'

'What is it?'

'Well, I don't know it exactly off by heart,' said Eric the Limp. 'I've got it written down.'

'Well we should try ringing it. We might hear it ring. Before we start tearing Nan's place apart.'

'For fart's sake, Tatts, she's not our Nan.'

'You are right of course,' said Tatts McIndoe patiently. 'But, please, Limpy, what is the number? Where did you write it down?'

'It'll be turned off.'

'You never know. What *is* the number?'

'I've got written down.'

'Where?'

'On my knee,' said Eric the Limp.

During this and the rest of the verbal exchange between the fraternal intruders the Widow Partridge sat quietly, her own cell phone now lying beside her on the couch, her hands in her lap twisting the handkerchief which she had retrieved from its home up the sleeve of her cardigan.

'You wrote the number on your knee?' asked an astonished Tatts McIndoe.

'On my knee,' said Eric the Limp. 'On my thigh actually. My left thigh. Above my knee.'

'Why is it written on that particularly obnoxious part of your anatomy?'

'Eh?'

'We – by that I mean normal people – usually write things like phone numbers on a piece of paper,' said Tatts McIndoe sarcastically.

Eric the Limp held up a warning forefinger. 'No need for sarcasm, Tatts,' he said. 'You said yourself. Look, I was on the dunny, if you must know, having a K – R – A – P – P, when one of Big Ben's savouries phoned me up hush-hush from The Lake and gave me the number.'

'She can spell, you know. She's not an idiot.'

'Actually it's a C,' said the Widow Partridge from her place on the couch. 'And one P.'

'What?' said the two men together, looking querulously at the Widow Partridge.

'It's C – R – A – P ,' said the Widow Partridge. 'In more ways than one actually,' she added.

'She is giving you a spelling lesson,' said Tatts McIndoe to his brother. 'Now, Limpy, the number please.'

'What?'

'We need the number, you idiot,' said Tatts McIndoe.

'I'll have to take my pants off,' said Eric the Limp. 'Tell your Nan to turn around.'

'She's not my Nan, Limpy, remember.'

'Just tell the old fart-bag to turn around.'

'I've seen a man's legs before you know,' said the Widow Partridge.

'Ponytail's skinny pegs?' said Eric the Limp. 'What a disgusting thought.'

'Just turn around, Nan,' said Tatts McIndoe gently.

And so, as Eric the Limp allowed his tight black trousers to fall to the axminster, the Widow Partridge turned her head aside only slightly.

'Now, Tatts,' said Eric the Limp. 'Use Nan's phone and call this number.'

The Widow Partridge willingly opened her phone again and handed it to Tatts McIndoe while Eric the Limp bent forward, turned his head awkwardly and called out the phone number printed in large figures in ball-point ink on the top of his left thigh just above the knee. Tatts McIndoe carefully pressed out the number.

'Of course, it is in the phone already,' he said as Ponytail's name and number appeared brightly on the screen. He listened. 'A message,' he said at last, holding the phone towards his partner.

'What sort of message?' asked Eric the Limp as he limpily shuffled and waddled across to his partner, his trousers around his ankles, his jacket and the tail of his white shirt not quite covering his baggy underpants. 'Put it on speaker.'

They listened to the end of the message being delivered by a cultured female voice.

'Standard Vodafone bullshit,' said Eric the Limp. 'The phone is turned off or blah blah humpty shit.' He bent down, pulled up his trousers, adjusted his shirt and jacket, and buckled his belt.

'Well, it is what one would expect under the circumstances,' said Tatts McIndoe. 'Why would he have his phone turned on if he's in hiding? But you never know. Now what?'

'You can turn around now, Nan,' said Eric the Limp to the Widow Partridge, much to her amusement. And then to his brother he said: 'Tear this shit-hole apart.'

'I do not believe that would be wise,' said Tatts McIndoe. 'Perhaps we should check it with Big Ben before we impose any further on Nan.'

'But, fart face, if the phone's hidden here somewhere she could get rid of it while we're checking with the boss.'

'Perhaps as may be,' said Tatts McIndoe thinkingly. 'But we've already hijacked her lift and smashed in her door. And you threatened her physically. An innocent old lady. We could be in enough trouble already. She knows our names and what we look like. She will probably call the long arm.' He turned to the Widow Partridge sitting patiently on the edge of the couch. 'You'll probably call the police, Nan, won't you.'

'Probably,' said the Widow Partridge calmly.

'Then what'll we do?'

'Let us simply leave here quietly while we can,' said Tatts McIndoe. 'Why ask for more trouble by ransacking her lovely abode?'

'Eh?'

'We do apologise for your door, Nan,' said Tatts McIndoe with a slight bow to the Widow Partridge. And then to his brother he beckoned and said quietly: 'Come here.'

Eric the Limp moved to the shorter man and put his right arm around his shoulder. Standing together like that they began and continued a whispering dialogue.

'Look, Limpy, this is a mess,' said Tatts McIndoe. 'We have nothing but trouble to gain from it all.'

'I don't get it,' said Eric the Limp.

'Why should we risk further trouble?' asked his brother.

'Eh?'

'From Big Ben or the long arm,' said Tatts McIndoe. 'The fact is she's probably telling the truth about Ponytail's phone. She probably posted it. Not remembered the address. Whatever. She's old. I don't think we have anything to gain by ransacking her flat. We can simply walk away from this. Tell Big Ben we tore her place apart but couldn't find it. How would he know better?'

'And why does he want it so much anyway?' asked Eric the Limp.

'Something about a recording,' said Tatts McIndoe. 'But I don't really know. Don't care really.'

'But what if it turns up somewhere else later.'

'Look, my brother,' said Tatts McIndoe. 'I think she probably posted it somewhere like Ponytail told her, like she said, where Ponytail could retrieve it when he gets out. We find Ponytail we find the phone. Simple.'

'So,' said Eric the Limp. 'Find Ponytail. Let's go.'

'But first let us sort Nan out,' said Tatts McIndoe.

'Eh?'

'I shall invite her into the conspiracy,' whispered Tatts McIndoe. 'I shall say that in return for us not ransacking her beautiful home, looking for Ponytail's phone, all she has to do if certain persons – viz Big Ben or anyone representing Big Ben – comes asking any awkward questions is say that we did indeed threaten her well-being, in fact she thought we might even kill her – exaggeration for effect – and we did indeed reduce her flat to a shambles in our search for the phone. In short she will report, to anyone who asks, that we were heartless and ruthless gangsters, thorough but ultimately unsuccessful in our search for Ponytail O'Gorman's phone.'

'You're a farting genius,' whispered Eric the Limp. 'Big Ben would like to hear that. But what about the long arm?'

'A *quid pro quo*,' said Tatts McIndoe.

'Eh?'

'A deal. A treaty. A contract. An agreement,' said Tatts McIndoe. 'We shall leave you and your flat alone, Nan, providing you promise not to call the long arm.'

'Or else,' whispered Eric the Limp as he removed his arm from around his brother's shoulders, slipped the cosh from the sleeve of his jacket and held it up threateningly in his right fist. 'But will she do it?'

'I believe we can trust the dear lady,' said Tatts McIndoe. 'Indeed, I'm sure we can.'

'Go on then,' said Eric the Limp as he returned the cosh to its sleevish home and pushed his brother towards the couch where the seated Widow Partridge waited patiently for the outcome of the whispered conference between the two young idiot thugs.

'Well, boys,' she said as she stood up. 'What have you decided to do to me and my crappy little flat?'

And when they were gone – when she had seen them below, looking ridiculous in their black ensembles on a sunny Oriental Parade, getting into one of the yellow Metlink buses which ran to town – she went to her desk phone and pressed out a well-remembered number.

'It's me,' she said quietly, calmly, after the recorded announcement and the beep. 'They've been here looking for Ponytail's phone. I'll tell you about it later, and about them, the stupid young fools, but the important thing is there's definitely something about a recording. Definitely Something.'

Chapter 9

'Home on a Monday,' said Paul-Frank to Faith. 'Feels funny.'

'Well, it's a holiday weekend, love, isn't it,' said Faith; it was the Wellington anniversary public holiday. 'Everyone's off today.'

'Not me usually. Usually had to blimmin work.'

'Sundays too. Often,' said Faith.

'But no more,' said Paul-Frank. 'Home all weekend every weekend. Even long weekends. And no shifts.'

'It's sooo nice, Pauly.'

Having Paul-Frank home for the long weekend, for *every* weekend, was something which his ten years of rotating shift work at Te Whareherehere, and before that in the army, had precluded for the thirteen years of the Ratanui's partnership. And on this sunny holiday Monday afternoon together – the beginning of the second week of Paul-Frank's pleasant, undemanding and stress-free new job in the number one permanent criminal court – they were sitting together in their sunny Kilbirnie back garden at their white garden table on matching garden chairs under the ancient persimmon tree enjoying tea and Faith's freshly-made scones (with strawberry jam and whipped cream). The moist scent of freshly-mown grass hung in the air.

'Short week this week, too,' said Paul-Frank

'Mmmm,' mmmmed Faith dreamily. 'Even better.'

'Do love my new job, love,' said Paul-Frank. 'So much variety it's amazing.'

Paul-Frank told Faith, as he had told Max Bridlington, that he enjoyed listening to the details of each trial, following the developing arguments of the prosecution and defence as they unfolded. But he didn't admit to Faith as he had to Max that he didn't understand anything about the corporate fraud trial which had opened on the Thursday and would resume the next day, Tuesday. And he didn't tell her what Max had told him about the Welly Alley Strangler; at least not the upsetting details. But he did mention it.

'Haven't had a murder yet,' he said. 'But there'll be a real doozie coming up before long Max said so that'll be good.'

'Doesn't sound good to me,' said Faith. 'Sounds horrible.'

'The Welly Alley Strangler he reckons,' said Paul-Frank.

'The Welly Alley Strangler? They've been after him for ages.'

'Well they've got him now apparently,' said Paul-Frank.

'No they haven't,' said Faith. 'I saw it in the paper.'

'Well, they know who he is anyway. They just have to find him.'

'How do you know that?'

'Max told me,' said Paul-Frank. 'Rumour around court.'

'A rumour?'

'He knows all the blimmin rumours,' said Paul-Frank. 'Seems to know lots of stuff.'

'But if it's only a rumour, Pauly?' said Faith.

She tried topping up their tea, holding down the teapot lid as she drained the last of the Choysa, but the teapot was empty. She put down the pot.

'You want more tea, love?'

'No, ta.'

'Another scone?'

'No, love,' said Paul-Frank holding up both hands in surrender. 'Enough. Honest.'

'This is *really* nice,' said Faith again before taking a bite from a new jam-and-cream-topped scone.

'The scone?' asked Paul-Frank.

'No, Pauly. I mean *this*,' she said after licking her lips clean of whipped cream. 'You and me together on a lovely holiday Monday afternoon.'

'Home every night,' said Paul-Frank.

'Same as me,' said Faith.

'Get the bus to town,' said Paul-Frank. 'There and back. Saves using the Land Cruiser, eh.'

'Mmmm,' mmmmed Faith.

'And home all weekend,' added Paul-Frank. 'That's the best.'

'And no fighting and violence,' said Faith. 'No stabbings. *That's* the best of all.'

'Nothing awful at all,' said Paul-Frank.

Faith finished her scone, wiped her mouth and hands on a serviette, and leaned back lazily in her chair, her hands clasped in her lap. She looked down the length of the short garden without actually seeing. She felt utterly content. Unbothered by anything.

'Know sometimes, love,' said Paul-Frank who also leaned back in his chair and clasped his meaty hands behind his big shaven head. 'Sometimes I recognize some of the crims in court. Evil, violent bastards some of them. But there, in the court, even the worst of them, in front of the judge and the jury and all the lawyers and stuff, they're so subdued. So quiet and meek. Afraid I suppose. Not like in The Lake.'

'I'm so glad there's no violence or anything, Pauly,' said Faith. 'It's hot today,' she added. 'Is it hot in the court?'

'Air-conditioned,' said Paul-Frank.

Faith felt remarkably relaxed sitting there in their back garden, in the shade of the old persimmon tree, on such a balmy holiday afternoon. She closed her eyes to better appreciate the moment and when she opened them she looked dreamily across the newly-mown lawn to Paul-Frank's ramshackle shed set against the unpainted wooden back fence which was charmingly old, rustic, somewhat rickety, and spotted with hairy grey-green lichen.

And then she saw something odd. Or, rather, she *thought* she saw something odd. Something that spoiled her peace of mind; made her sit up uneasily. She resented her holiday serenity being spoiled by, what? She didn't know what.

'You *did* do the lawns didn't you, Pauly?' she asked from her sitting-up-straight position without taking her eyes off the shed.

Paul-Frank looked across at her oddly, slightly sideways, as if to ask what's this about? 'Yes,' he answered somewhat tentatively. 'This morning. Isn't it obvious?'

'You put the mower away? In the shed?'

'Yes. Course I did, love. What are you looking at?'

Faith turned around. 'I thought I saw something – someone – moving in the shed. The little window.'

'Impossible,' said Paul-Frank.

'I don't know,' said Faith with doubt. 'It's just that–'

Paul-Frank dropped his hands to his lap and turned to follow Faith's gaze; he peered squintingly down the back garden to the shed at the end. He saw nothing untoward.

'Locked the shed, love.' Even at a distance he could see the bulky brass-and-steel padlock hanging, locked, as he had left it. 'No one can get in there without breaking down the door,' he said. 'Or breaking the blimmin window.'

'Must be my imagination,' said Faith doubtfully. 'But I'm sure I–'

Paul-Frank returned his hands to their clasped position behind his head. '*Is* a lovely day, love,' he said brightly.

'I know,' said Faith who relaxed back into her chair but nevertheless felt eerily but inexplicably unsettled.

Half an hour later Paul-Frank went indoors to use the toilet while Faith prepared to clear the garden table and return the tea things to the kitchen. And as she fussed at the table, in the cool shade of the old persimmon tree, she couldn't help but pause and glance back at the little and almost-derelict unpainted wooden shed with a rusty tin roof that stood at the end of the garden; and she couldn't help squinting, and wondering, as she peered at the blackness behind the small dusty window which was hung with a dirty, ragged and unmoving lace curtain.

Chapter 10

'What the hell?'

Gentle Paul-Frank Ratanui didn't get angry often but he was angry now.

Faith could walk home from the bank so she got home first.

'How was your day, Pauly love?' she asked Paul-Frank when he got home. 'The start of your second week and only four days.'

Paul-Frank leaned down and kissed his little wife affectionately on the cheek.

'Fine, love,' he said. 'Just fine. Yours?'

'Oh, Pauly, it was fine too,' said Faith. 'Except–' she added.

But Paul-Frank didn't notice her hesitation. 'Tea in the pot?' he asked.

'Plenty,' said Faith.

'Have a cup I think.'

'But, Pauly, before you do.'

'What?'

'I'm sorry, love, but when I got home. Well, the thing is, could you check the shed?'

'Eh?'

'Pauly, I'm sorry, I know you think I'm silly, but I'm sure there's someone – or something – in the shed.'

And now a reluctant Paul-Frank – having unlocked and removed the heavy-duty brass-and-steel padlock from the latch on the shed door, and opened the said shed door – was standing in the open doorway staring at the unkempt and dishevelled little intruder sitting stiff and straight and nervous and guilty-looking on the edge of the dusty old armchair in which he himself liked to sit and relax in private with a cold beer after mowing the lawns and/or working in the garden. Indeed, he had every intention of pottering about in the garden after dinner on this fine summer's evening. A Tuesday. And now this. Now he was angry.

'The hell are you doing here?' he asked again. Angrily.

'Oh, stink! I'm sorry, Mr R, I really am, eh,' said Ponytail O'Gorman, for that of course was the identity of the shed intruder.

Paul-Frank ignored the apology. 'And how did you find out where I live?'

At that Ponytail stood up, smiled smugly and shrugged as if to ask: you really have to ask an old con a dumb question like that?

'Jeez,' said Paul-Frank in frustration. 'Have you been sleeping here?'

'Mr R. Please. I got nowhere else to go.'

'Eh? Last time I heard you were in hospital recovering from that stab wound.'

'That was stink, eh,' said Ponytail.

'So how'd you blimmin get here.'

'The wae wae express,' said Ponytail as he sat down again.

'You *walked* all the way from the hospital to here?'

'I got no stinkin money, Mr R,' said Ponytail. 'I had to walk, eh.'

'Oh, Jeez, Ponytail,' said a suddenly miserable Paul-Frank, wretched with guilt. 'You poor bastard. I'm so sorry for spewing all over you.'

'Eh?'

'Never had the chance to say it properly,' said Paul-Frank. 'I'm so sorry, man.'

'Foo, that's alright, Mr R,' said Ponytail brightly. 'You're totally forgiven and forgotten.'

'Thank you so much, man,' said Paul-Frank humbly.

'I recovered didn't I,' said Ponytail turning his hands inwards and pointing at his chest. 'Look at me, bro. Sweet as. Bloody glowing with it if you know what I mean. Picture of it, eh.'

'Look a bloody mess to me,' said Paul-Frank. 'A dog's breakfast.'

Ponytail did indeed look like the proverbial canine's morning meal. His jeans, yellow t-shirt and sneakers were grubby, as was his thin and little person; and he needed a shave. He looked like a tramp, a homeless person, which indeed he was as he had just confessed.

But he ignored the comment on his appearance and instead responded boldly and bluntly: 'But now you owe me, bro.'

His guilt somewhat relieved, Paul-Frank's anger returned. 'What do you mean?'

'For the spew. You owe me.'

'Come on,' said an incredulous Paul-Frank. 'You just said—'

'Only joking, bro,' said the grubby little intruder with a grin. 'But I need your help, eh. I really do truly.'

'Oh, mate,' said Paul-Frank. 'What can *I* do?'

'Heaps,' said Ponytail. 'I'll tell you.'

'But how come you're here?' asked Paul-Frank. 'How come you're out of The Lake?'

'I got better and got parole while I was in that stink hospital so I didn't have to go back,' said Ponytail. 'They let me out from the hospital. Compassionate they said.'

'You're better? From that stabbing?'

'Tolja, didn't I,' said Ponytail. 'Fit as a fiddle. Box of budgies. And free as a bird.'

'On parole you said.'

'On parole, no worries,' confirmed Ponytail. 'So, Mr R–' at this point Ponytail held out his grubby hands, palms up, as if ready to accept a gift '–where is it?'

'Where's what?'

'The phone,' said Ponytail.

'What phone?' Paul-Frank was genuinely puzzled.

'The stinkin phone the Widow Partridge sent you? Posted by the post office.'

'What the hell's the Widow Partridge got to do with anything?'

'I gave her the stinkin phone in the infirmary when I was there and she posted it to you,' said a suddenly worried and doubtful Ponytail.

'Mate,' said Paul-Frank gently; he sensed Ponytail's rising alarm. 'I don't know what you're talking about. Honest.'

'Stee-yink!' said Ponytail. 'That was – what? – more than two weeks ago, man. Shoulda had it by now.' He sat on the arm of the dusty old armchair, and looked up at Paul-Frank quizzically. 'Are you one hundred percent stinkin sure you aint got it? The phone? A little black cell phone in the post?'

'Ponytail, my friend,' said Paul-Frank, 'honestly don't know what the hell you're talking about.'

'Foo, something's gone seriously stinkin wrong as wrong, eh,' said Ponytail. He slumped back into the depths of the dusty old armchair shaking his head worriedly. 'Dead wrong if you know what I mean.'

'But how did you get in here anyway?' asked Paul-Frank leaning forward and holding the bulky padlock in front of the grubby little homeless man who was almost lost in the depths of the big and dusty old armchair. 'This is my shed, man. My private property.'

'Don't panic, Mr R. I aint touched nothing,' said Ponytail reassuringly. And then, looking around, he added: 'Bit of dump anyway, bro.'

'My shed,' said Paul-Frank indignantly. 'All my own and I like it.'

'What's that thing?'

'Exercise machine I bought once. Lose weight.'

'Didn't work, bro,' said Ponytail with a toothy giggle that opened his mouth and almost closed his eyes.

Paul-Frank ignored him. 'But how did you get in?' he asked again.

Once again the little man smiled and shrugged as if to ask: you really have to ask an old con a dumb question like that?

'And what are you doing here anyway? It looks like you've been sleeping here.'

'I come to get the phone,' said Ponytail. 'I thought you'd figure out I was here and come and give me the phone.'

'Eh?'

'I can't sort out anything about Simple Simon and that till then.'

'Till when? Jeez, man, you're talking in riddles,' said Paul-Frank in utter confusion and frustration. 'And what's Simple Simon got to do with it?'

Paul-Frank knew Simple Simon as a petty crook – a bit of a simpleton, hence his nickname – from his few short spells in The Lake.

'Oh, it's stink, Mr R, it really is,' said Ponytail. He stood up and looked up at Paul-Frank. 'Specially without the phone. I've gotta hide. I'm on the stinkin run.'

'Jeez, you're on parole, man. What the hell have you done now?'

'It's not the long arm, bro. I'm as free as a bird as far as the long arm's concerned. Waddya think I am?'

'I think you're an old con; a crook,' said Paul-Frank.

'Such a stinkin cynic,' said Ponytail. 'A fellah can go straight you know, bro.'

'So what's going on?'

'A certain person – not the long arm – is after me, Mr R, for a certain real stink reason. So I've gotta hide till I find the phone. I got nowhere else to stay sept here.'

'Well that's not on,' said Paul-Frank firmly. 'Missus'll go mad. So how long have you been here anyway?'

'Just three nights, Mr R,' whimpered an obsequious and untruthful Ponytail. 'Three nights is all only. Honest.'

'Jeez. And how do you–'

'If you must know, bro, there's a choice wharepaku in the shopping centre,' said Ponytail. 'Clean. Stainless steel from top to bottom. You aint never seen nothing so clean if you know what I mean. And a Burger King.'

'But you said you've got no money.'

'Who needs money at Burger King?' said Ponytail.

'Surprised they even let you in to Burger King looking like that.'

'They don't,' said Ponytail. 'I go to the drive-in window. I know the girl there, eh. Cousin on my mother's side.'

'Told me once you were an orphan.'

'Hey! Doesn't mean I didn't have a mother once,' said Ponytail in indignation. 'Or aunties or cousins. Man, my whanau. Got heaps of cousins, eh. Heaps and heaps of them all over the stinkin place.'

'Jeez, I don't know, Ponytail,' said Paul-Frank with a sigh. He looked back to the house, through the shed window, worried that Faith might be worried and might come down to the shed and find him talking to Ponytail. 'You just can't blimmin stay here anymore. You just can't.'

'I know that, eh, Mr R,' said Ponytail. He climbed onto the seat of the armchair to be closer to Paul-Frank's height. 'I don't mean to be a stink and that, and I'll go soon, but I'll have to go back to the Widow Partridge and find out where she sent the phone but I can't if you know what I mean.'

'Why not?'

'They'll be watching her place for sure, man.'

'Who?' asked Paul-Frank. Logically. 'Who'll be watching her place?'

'I know,' said Ponytail, more to himself. 'I'll ring her up.'

'Who'll be watching her place?' asked Paul-Frank again.

Ponytail, still standing on the seat of the old armchair, stretched his arms forward, rested his hands on Paul-Frank's broad shoulders, looked deeply into his black eyes, and said grimly: 'A certain bad fellah with a stink attitude and two real bad friends is out to get me and my cell phone,' he said mysteriously. 'And if you aint got it and the Widow Partridge aint got it then me and Simple Simon are deep in the stink-pot if you know what I mean. Without a paddle or nothing, eh.'

'Eh?' queried Paul-Frank. 'I still don't know what Simple Simon's got to do with it.'

'Everything, Mr R. Stinkin everything. If I can't find the phone then me and him will really be in the poo-pond. We'll need your help big time then for sure, we really will.'

'Help? What sort of help?'

'Protection.'

'Protection?'

'Yeah, man. Like a body guard.'

'Body guard. Me? Jeez, get outa here. No way.'

'It's stink I know,' said Ponytail. 'But I don't know where else to turn?'

'But why me? What can I do?'

'Come on, Mr R,' said Ponytail. 'Look at the size of you. A stinkin giant among men. A colossusus they reckon in The Lake. Everyone there's afraid of you, eh. Your size and strength. You looked after me in that stinkin place so why shouldn't you look after me out here? Only natural.'

'Not a bit natural,' said a frustrated Paul-Frank. 'In there they were afraid of me. Can't you see? In there I had the uniform, the helmet, the boots, the truncheon, the radio, and mostly the power and authority of the whole New Zealand C and C department behind me. And they were prisoners. You too. Powerless prisoners. Nowhere to go. No one to turn to. But that was there, man. Can't you see? Outside, now, here, have no more power than anyone else.'

'Waddya mean now? Outside? You mean you aint in The Lake no more?'

'No more,' confirmed Paul-Frank.

'Got the royal order of the boot, eh,' said Ponytail with a chuckle.

'Did not,' said Paul-Frank firmly. 'I left. Couldn't stand it anymore.'

'So waddya do now? On the dole, eh. Another WINZ winner.'

'No way. Work in security at the number one permanent criminal court in town if it's any of your business which it isn't.'

'Doesn't matter to me, Mr R,' said Ponytail. 'You've still got your size, bro, and stinkin big muscles, to protect me.'

'Simple Simon can protect you,' said Paul-Frank. 'He's a huge bugger. Why don't you ask him to protect you?'

'Don't know where he is,' said Ponytail. 'But, anyway, he's big and nice but dumb as. He needs my brains to protect him from his own dumbness if you know what I mean. Actually, when I find him we're both gonna need you, Mr R.'

'No way, man,' insisted Paul-Frank. 'A wimp really. Can't stand violence. Look how I spewed all over you when you got stabbed. All that blood of yours.'

'I'd rather forget that,' said Ponytail with a grimace.

'Who did that, by the way?' asked Paul-Frank. 'Stabbed you? They never found out.'

'Can't say,' said Ponytail. 'My lips are totally sealed.'

'*Won't* say,' said Paul-Frank.

Ponytail shrugged. 'Doesn't matter no more if you know what I mean,' he said.

'Look, Ponytail,' said Paul-Frank firmly. 'This is the real world. And I'm as afraid of violence and ruthless criminals as anyone.'

'But, stink, Mr R, aint no one else,' said Ponytail. 'No one cares about me and Simple Simon.'

'The Widow Partridge does,' said Paul-Frank somewhat flippantly.

'That's true, Mr R,' said Ponytail seriously. 'Me and her are getting married when this is over.'

'See,' said Paul-Frank.

'But that's wahine care, man,' said Ponytail. 'Aroha. It's choice I know. But it aint no protection against crims like Big Ben.'

'But Big Ben's in The Lake,' said Paul-Frank. 'He can't get you. Not for a couple of years anyway.'

'What about them brothers,' said Ponytail. 'They scare the hot piss outa me.'

'Who?' asked Paul-Frank. 'Limpy and Tatts?'

'That's them,' said Ponytail. 'They do whatever Big Ben tells them, the dirty stinkin rats.'

'Get down,' said Paul-Frank. He lifted Ponytail bodily off the seat of the old armchair and pushed him back to a sitting position deep in the armchair's dusty depths where the grubby little man looked tiny and lost; he looked up at Paul-Frank pathetically.

'They're after me because–'

But Paul-Frank held out his right arm, hand up, like a policeman stopping traffic. 'Stop!' he said.

'What?'

'Don't want to know,' said Paul-Frank, dropping his arm.

'Stink, Mr R,' said Ponytail. 'How do you know you don't want to know.'

'Just blimmin know I don't want to know don't I,' said Paul-Frank. 'So shut up, okay? Just shut up.'

'But Simple Simon, bro,' pleaded Ponytail. 'He's a friend of mine, see, and they're after him next. For something he never even done. I don't know what they'll do to him.'

And then, from a distance, from the house, they both heard Faith calling from the back porch: 'Are you alright there, love?'

'Your missus,' said Ponytail in mild alarm. He got out of the chair and looked ready to flee.

'Yeah,' said Paul-Frank. 'You've gotta go. And so do I.' And then he turned, pushed the shed door half open and held it there as he called in reply: 'Won't be a minute, love.'

'Foo, that was close, eh,' said Ponytail.

'Too close for comfort,' said Paul-Frank as he shut the door. 'I'll have to go. And so will you. Now.'

'But if we need help, me and Simon, will you help us?' asked Ponytail.

'How can I help?' said Paul-Frank, his arms held forward, his hands palms up, questioningly.

'I'll be in touch, Mr R. Later.'

'How?' asked Paul-Frank. 'And when? And where are you going now?'

But Ponytail was gone. He had quickly and quietly slipped out the same open back window of the shed through which he had previously slipped in. Paul-Frank looked blankly at the big and bulky brass-and-steel padlock he still held in his right hand.

'Anything?' asked Faith when Paul-Frank returned to the kitchen. 'You were ages.'

'A bag of blood and bone was tipped over.'

'Is that all?'

'I think there's been a rat in the shed,' said Paul-Frank.

Chapter 11

Later that night the Widow Partridge received a call on her cell phone from Ponytail O'Gorman to whom she had been assigned as official visitor when and while he had been confined at Te Whareherehere prison. She had been worried about him since she had learned from Tatts McIndoe and his brother that he had been released not only from the care of the hospital but altogether from prison custody and so she was relieved to hear from him at last. It was the first she had heard from him since she had gone with him to the hospital; that followed her earlier visit to the infirmary where and when he had secretly returned the little cell phone to her, she who had smuggled it into the prison and given it to him in the first place.

'But where are you, Ponytail dear?' she asked. 'I heard you were out of hospital. Out of prison and everything.'

'That's right, Rosie. I'm free as.'

'But where are you? Are you alright? It's so late.'

'Oh, Rosie, I'm using a stinkin pay-phone outside Burger King. I just had a burger. They're closing.'

'I don't understand,' said the Widow Partridge. 'What Burger King? Where? In town or what?'

'I can't tell you that, Rosie,' said Ponytail. 'Anyway, that doesn't matter.'

'But you're *really* out of hospital?'

'Yeah, Rosie, out of hospital and out of The Lake. They let me go. Compassionate they said. On parole.'

'Oh, how wonderful,' said the Widow Partridge. She was genuinely pleased for her crooked little friend. 'But are you all right?' she asked again. 'Your wound?'

'Oh, Rosie, it was nothing,' said Ponytail. 'Nothing at all if you know what I mean.'

'It didn't seem like nothing to me.'

'I'm a ball of muscle,' said Ponytail. 'Sweet as. Hunky-dory. A box of budgies, eh.'

'Really?'

'I'm fine, Rosie, if you know what I mean. Just fine.'

'But where are you stopping?' asked the worried widow.

'I can't tell you that neither, Rosie,' said Ponytail. 'Not yet. They might be listening, eh.'

'Who?' asked the Widow Partridge. 'Who might be listening?'

'Don't you worry about that. I'm hiding somewhere safe where they can't find me. Never will.'

'You mean those two young boy-thugs don't you,' said the Widow Partridge.

'Stink! You know about them?'

'Maybe they can't find *you*, dear,' said the Widow Partridge, 'but they jolly well found *me*.'

'Stink, no! You mean Big Ben's boys?'

'Yes. Two young idiots. No more than children.'

'That's Tatts and Limpy. What happened?'

'They wanted your phone.'

'What did you tell them?'

'I told them I posted it like you told me to,' said the Widow Partridge.

'Stee-yink, Rosie. What did you do that for? And anyway that's the problem. I checked. Mr R never got it.'

'It's alright, Ponytail,' said the Widow Partridge.

'No it's not,' said Ponytail. 'It means they'll be after Mr Ratanui now.'

'No they won't, dear,' said the widow. 'I told them I just copied the address you gave me and couldn't remember what it was.'

'They believed you?'

'Oh, Ponytail, I don't know,' said the Widow Partridge. 'I think so. But they really are a couple of young idiots.'

'True. But the thing is, Rosie, it still hasn't arrived if you know what I mean. The phone,' said Ponytail.

'So you're stopping with Mr Ratanui,' said Mrs Partridge and it wasn't a question. 'The prison guard.'

'Yes. No,' said Ponytail quickly. 'Well, not zactly if you know what I mean.'

'Don't you worry, Ponytail dear,' said Mrs Partridge. 'I won't tell anyone.'

'It's not that,' protested Ponytail. 'It's been more than two weeks hasn't it. Two whole stinkin weeks.'

'What's been two weeks?'

'Since you posted the stinkin phone.'

'The phone is fine,' said Mrs Partridge. 'Quite safe.'

'How come?'

'Because, Ponytail dear,' said Mrs Partridge. 'I had a funny feeling about it so I didn't post it to Mr Ratanui like you said.'

'So what did you do with it?' Ponytail was alarmed.

'I posted it somewhere else.'

'Where?'

'Somewhere secret,' said Mrs Partridge. 'Somewhere no one will find it.'

'Stink, Rosie. Tell me now,' said Ponytail. 'I done what you asked – much more actually – and now I need it bad.'

'Listen, dear,' said the Widow Partridge. 'If it's about the photo, what does it matter? Big Ben knows Simon was with me on new year's eve. He's even got a copy of the photo from *my* phone.'

'Eh?'

'They made me open my phone and they sent the photo of me and Simon to the little fat one's phone.'

'Tatts's phone. Why'd they do that?'

'So they could show it to Big Ben again they said,' said the Widow Partridge.

'But he's already seen it when I stinkin showed it to him,' said Ponytail. 'That's how Big Ben knew that Simple Simon was with you on new year's eve.'

'I know *that*. Maybe Big Ben wants his own copy. To be sure or something. Anyway they deleted it from my phone. I haven't got it anymore.'

'Oh, stink. They really deleted the photo from your phone.'

'I'm afraid so,' said the Widow Partridge.

'Well, it'll still be on my phone wherever it is,' said Ponytail. 'But there's something else,' he added.

'Did you get a recording?' asked the Widow Partridge tentatively. 'Those two idiots seem to know something about a sound file or something. Did you get something? Did it work?'

'It worked. But stink, they must know,' said a horrified and terrified Ponytail. 'That's why Big Ben's so desperate.'

'So you *did* get something,' said the Widow Partridge, more to herself. And then to Ponytail she added: 'So if those two young idiots find you they'll want the phone but if you haven't got it, and you honestly don't know where it is, then they won't get their hands on it will they.'

'They'll get their hands on me and my skinny neck, Rosie. What about that? They'll stinkin torture me to death or worse even.'

'No they won't,' said the Widow Partridge dismissively; confidently. 'They're a couple of stupid young cowards. All mouth and trousers as my mother used to say. And dirty boots. And anyway I'm sure Mr Ratanui will look after you.'

'I don't even know about that now,' said Ponytail.

'You never should have shown that photo of me and Simon to anyone, dear,' said the Widow Partridge in gentle admonishment. 'You *do* know that now don't you?'

'Well you shouldn't have stinkin sent it to me and all that,' replied Ponytail in his own gentle admonishment.

'If we – if I'd – have known–' said the Widow Partridge. 'But let's not argue about that now.'

'No. I'm just so stinkin sorry about it all, eh,' said Ponytail. 'And what about Simon? He's in a big stink now cause of me. Do you know where he is?'

'No. But I'm sure he's fine,' said the Widow Partridge reassuringly.

But Ponytail was not to be reassured so easily.

'How do you know that for totally sure? You don't know that.'

'I'm sure he'll be fine.'

'Oh, Rosie, I'm so stinkin worried about him,' he said. 'He such a big dummy. If Big Ben's boys finds him he'll be dead for sure.'

'Truly, don't worry, dear,' said the Widow Partridge with a strange and knowing confidence. 'They won't find him. I'm sure of that.'

'But he double-crossed Big Ben,' said Ponytail. 'No one in the world does that. Not never ever. If Tatts and Limpy—'

'They *won't* find him, dear,' said Mrs Partridge confidently. 'I'm sure they won't. They really are a couple of complete idiots.'

'But, Rosie,' said an increasingly worried Ponytail. 'You've just got to get me that stinkin phone. Could be a matter of life and death or worse. Please, Rosie,' he begged.

'I'll see what I can do, dear,' said the Widow Partridge. 'Meanwhile don't you worry. About the phone or Simon or anything.'

'Easy for you to say if you know what I mean.'

'Phone me again when you can,' said the Widow Partridge. 'I'll see what I can do.'

And when that conversation was over – and as Ponytail left the Burger King car park heading through the night for his shed home in Kilbirnie – his widowed friend made a call of her own, from her desk phone, to the same unmanned number she had called before.

'It's me again,' she said quietly. 'There's definitely a recording. Could be what you need. Ponytail's secretive about it but he's really worried.'

The innocuous little black cell phone to which the Widow Partridge referred, being so eagerly sought by Tatts McIndoe and Eric the Limp (on behalf of Big Ben Pye), and of course by Ponytail himself, lay at that moment on the kitchen counter of a two-storied brick and tile homestead at the address in faraway Martinborough to which the Widow Partridge had posted it immediately she had received it in the infirmary from the wounded Ponytail. It lay harmlessly on its back on the counter of the dark kitchen beside the kettle, tea pot and a tin tea caddy whose lid bore a somewhat scratched colour photo of Windsor Castle, which stood together domestically, suburbanly, innocently, beside a big Kelvinator refrigerator/freezer. It was of course turned off; the phone, that is, not the refrigerator/freezer. It, the refrigerator/freezer, was full of food and drink sufficient, without replenishment, to sustain two people for a month or more.

Chapter 12

All Big Ben knew at the beginning was that on new year's eve Simple Simon had been at a party somewhere – it could have been anywhere – with the Widow Partridge. He knew it was new year's eve from the "Happy New Year" banner and the lights and bunting in the background of the photo which Ponytail O'Gorman had foolishly shown him on his phone in an attempt to flaunt his intimate friendship with the rich Widow Partridge.

But he *now* knew that the party had been a public affair held at the Martinborough Hotel in the Wairarapa. He knew that now because Tatts McIndoe and Eric the Limp had told him because the Widow Partridge had told them. And that, reasoned Big Ben, meant that the Simple Simon partying in Martinborough on new year's eve couldn't have carried out the contract in distant Wellington for which he had been paid twenty-five hundred dollars in advance. And if Simple Simon hadn't fulfilled his contract then not only did he, Big Ben, stand to lose twenty-five hundred dollars but, he also reasoned, someone – an evil murdering bastard he called him – had done what Simple Simon was supposed to have done; and whoever *that* was would now get undeserved credit for the entire series of meticulously planned and expertly executed murders for which he, Benjamin Cedric Pye, was entirely and solely responsible and of which he was necessarily secretly but inordinately proud. That Simple Simon should have done it under his instructions was acceptable; that someone he didn't know had done it and would take the credit for the complete series was entirely unacceptable at least in his twisted view of what was and was not acceptable behaviour.

'How dare he,' he said angrily to his two remarkably innocent apprentice henchboys who were visiting him that Wednesday afternoon and had imparted what they had learned from the Widow Partridge, the previous Sunday, of the new year's eve party's remote location. 'The evil murdering bastard. Taking all the credit. I'll fucking kill him.'

'Who? Taking the credit for what?' asked Tatts McIndoe naively.

'Never you mind what that's what,' said Big Ben angrily.

'We're not with you, boss,' said Eric the Limp nervously.

'I mean if *he* didn't do it–'

'Do what?' asked a puzzled Tatts McIndoe. 'Who?'

'You *did* fucking give him the dough didn't you?'

'Who? Simple Simon? Of course we did,' said Tatts McIndoe indignantly.

'But he was at that fucking party wasn't he, the prick,' said Big Ben who was getting hotter under his non-existent collar with every sentence uttered. 'Way up in Martinborough. The Rimutakas.'

'You mean the photo,' said Tatts McIndoe. 'Ponytail's photo.'

Big Ben ignored the young brothers – he seemed to have forgotten where he was, what he was saying, and that they were even there – and rambled on loudly, aggressively, almost incoherently. 'So if he never done it on new year's eve,' he rambled, 'then some other bastard done it and is taking *all* the fucking credit for *all* of them.'

Suddenly it – it being the subject to which Big Ben was referring – dawned on Tatts McIndoe with a frightening clarity.

'You don't mean that *you*–' said the astonished boy aghastly.

'Eh?' said Eric the Limp as he looked first at his brother, then at the angry red face of his boss who was sitting across the table from them, and then at the truth which was now staring him in his youthful, pasty, pock-marked and whiskerless face.

'Forget that,' said Big Ben dismissively as the proverbial bee, big and angry as it was, slowly departed his bonnet. 'Just find Ponytail O'Gorman and get that phone–'

'But–' interrupted Tatts McIndoe.

'Shut the fuck up and listen,' said Big Ben, his red-faced anger returning.

Tatts McIndoe swallowed with fright and shut up as requested; his brother looked on silently.

'Then find Simple Simon and get my dough back,' said Big Ben. Then he sighed deeply and suddenly sounded tired.

'You mean you paid him, *we* paid him, to–' Tatts McIndoe was now fully horrified.

'What the wet fart!' said Eric the Limp eloquently as his uptake equipment managed to click into gear after its customary sluggish start.

'I said forget it,' insisted Big Ben. 'Just find O'Gorman and Simple Simon. Get me the phone and my dough. Kill them if you have to. Kill them both. I don't care.'

'Kill them?' said a suddenly very frightened Tatts McIndoe. He'd never heard Big Ben talk like that before. Never seen him so angry before.

'Look, you dumb dicks, the phone and the dough. That's it. Do it!' insisted Big Ben again.

'But we don't know where they are,' said Eric the Limp. 'Honest, boss.'

'They're probably in it together the bastards,' said Big Ben, more to himself than to his companions.

'In what?' asked Tatts McIndoe. But it was an entirely rhetorical question designed to furnish him with thinking time while he pondered his options; he now pretty-well knew for sure what the it was that Big Ben believed Ponytail and Simple Simon were together in. For Big Ben though the question was the last straw. Suddenly, without warning, he stood up, his anger erupting loudly.

'I just want that fucking cell phone,' he shouted. 'I don't care what you do, or who you do it to, or how, just get me that phone or else,' at which point in his increasingly loud declamation he showed his teeth and drew his flattened podgy right hand slowly, horizontally, across his thick throat in the universal and timeless gesture the implication of which Tatts McIndoe and Eric the Limp did not fail to grasp.

In that they were not alone: the C and C prison officer superintending the Te Whareherehere visiting hall at that time saw one of the prison's most undesirable inmates stand up – that was forbidden – and recognized the gesture he was making to his two dopey-looking adolescent visitors, and arbitrarily interpreted it, in accordance with his warrant, as unacceptable behaviour. As a result the by-now out-of-control red-faced offender was immediately returned to his cell – angrily lashing out at and cursing the officers who forcibly escorted him – while his two visitors, whom the prison officer in question assumed to be the prisoner's sons, or even grandsons so young did they look, were roughly, unceremoniously, ejected from the visiting hall and escorted out of the prison by two burly C and C guards.

'Jesus farting Christ that was a bit scary,' said Eric the Limp whose uptake equipment was now fully functioning.

He and his brother were standing on Taharoto Street in the shadow of Te Whareherehere's towering castellated stone walls and beside its solid iron gate on that Wednesday afternoon, brushing themselves down physically and metaphorically.

'Holy shit, yes,' said Tatts McIndoe from whose mouth words having a scatological etymology rarely came.

'So now what?' asked his anxious brother.

'Now what indeed,' was the nervous and unknowing reply.

Chapter 13

Earlier that day, in the staff canteen of the number one permanent criminal court on the Court Road, Paul-Frank Ratanui and his colleague Max Bridlington were having lunch.

'Prisoner duty next week,' said Max.

The following Monday would be the first day of Paul-Frank's first fortnight on prisoner duty which meant that for the following two weeks, rather than guarding the court doors, he and his senior partner would be responsible for escorting the prisoners to and from the basement cells and standing with them in the dock for the duration of each court session.

'Sounds a bit boring,' said Paul-Frank. 'Just looking out into the court – the judge and all the others, and the jury – or at the back of prisoners' heads.'

'I don't mind it,' said Max. 'You can see the judge up close, and watch the barristers and solicitors and clerks at work. Talking to each other. Watching the jury opposite is interesting too.'

They each had a mince-and-cheese pie – liberally tomato-sauced – which they were eating with the knives and forks which canteen decorum demanded but which they both wished they could eat from their hands. They each also had a milky cup of tea waiting at two o'clock to the pie plate.

Trying to sound nonchalant Paul-Frank asked Max, casually, as if in passing, between mouthfuls of pie: 'Heard any more about the Alley Strangler business, Max?'

And Max, his mouth full of mince, cheese, and saucy flaky pastry, some light dry flakes of which were escaping from the moist and sticky grip of his lips and floating down to the green Formica table-top, shook his head as if to say wait until I've finished this mouthful.

Paul-Frank waited.

At last Max swallowed, licked his lips, rinsed his mouth with hot tea, and said, in proper reply: 'It was only a rumour, Pauly. I haven't heard any more. Why?'

'Just interested,' said Paul-Frank. 'It'll be my first murder.'

'I see,' said Max. 'But even if the rumour's true a trial will be a long way off.'

'You thought they'd arrested someone or were going to arrest someone or something like that,' said Paul-Frank trying to sound merely curious but actually sounding quite anxious.

But old Max Bridlington was not fooled. He paused, his fork – the next piece of meaty pie waiting on its tines – poised in the air.

'It was only a rumour, Pauly,' he said dismissively. 'Tenny-rate, don't worry about it.'

He watched his partner to judge his reaction but Paul-Frank looked back blankly, passively.

They finished their lunch in silence; at least silence between them although the canteen was full of people and hence full of people-talking-noise and the clutter-clatter of crockery and the tinny clink of cutlery and glassware. And then, their plates pushed aside, Max took a last swig of tea, leaned back in his chair and said to a still-worried-looking Paul-Frank: 'There's something on your mind, Pauly, isn't there.'

'Fraid so,' admitted Paul-Frank.

'Well, come on,' said Max.

And so, in the time available before having to resume their duties in the courtroom, Paul-Frank leaned across the table and spoke quietly – almost whisperingly – to his partner who had to lean forward across the table to better hear the story being so softly told.

'Remember I told you about a small-time con man called Ponytail O'Gorman?'

'Of course,' said Max. 'Ponytail. The bloke who got stabbed in The Lake? The bloke you vomited all over?'

Paul-Frank grimaced with embarrassment. 'Yeah, him,' he said.

'What about him?'

'Thing is, he's out now,' said Paul-Frank. 'Actually he never went back to The Lake but got released from hospital. On parole apparently. But the thing is he came to see me.'

'Where?'

'My place.'

'That's weird,' said Max. 'An ex-con visiting an ex-screw at home.'

'In my shed actually,' said Paul-Frank. 'Secretly. Was hiding there. Still is I think. Nowhere to go. Think he's on the run.'

'Already? I'm not surprised.'

'No, no,' said Paul-Frank defensively. 'It's not the police. Says he hasn't done anything. Says someone's after him. Real bad bastard I know called Big Ben who was in The Lake with him. Still there in fact.'

'I remember him in court,' said Max. 'Last year.'

'That'd be right,' said Paul-Frank. 'Well somehow Ponytail's also involved with another stupid crook, a bloke I know vaguely from The Lake called Simple Simon.'

'Funny name,' said Max. 'What's his real name?'

'Don't rightly know,' said Paul-Frank, anxious to get on. 'Doesn't matter about that. Thing is, I don't why, it's just a feeling you know, but I reckon Ponytail knows something about the new year's eve murder of that mysterious girl. The Welly Alley Strangler murder. That somehow his mate Simple Simon's involved. I don't know how or why. But Simple Simon's such a big bastard. And strong. He could easily–'

'Wow,' said Max Bridlington. 'Really? But what makes you think that?'

'Don't know,' said Paul-Frank honestly. 'Just a blimmin strange feeling.'

'I understand,' said Max. 'A feeling. Tenny-rate, tell me more.'

'Well, Ponytail reckons his visitor, his official prison visitor you know, a lady they all call the Widow Partridge, was supposed to have posted a cell phone to me with something on it that he needs, I don't know what, but it never arrived, not yet anyway and it should have by now, and now Big Ben wants it too and so he's on the run from Big Ben and so is Simple Simon and he wants my help.'

'Who? Simple Simon?'

'No. Ponytail,' said Paul-Frank. 'And, yes, maybe Simple Simon. I don't know about that.'

'But you said this Big Ben's in The Lake.'

'He is,' said Paul-Frank. 'But he's got a couple of dogsbodies outside. Treacherous young bastards they are. Ponytail's terrified of them and they're out to get him and this phone of his. Only he hasn't got it and neither have I and he doesn't know where it is or what to do and he's scared shitless.'

'Let me get this straight, Pauly,' said Max, quietly, when Paul-Frank was finished. They were still huddled together across the table. 'You think – you're guessing, you've got a funny feeling or something, from what your little ex-con mate Ponytail told you, or *didn't* tell you – that this Simple Simon chap could have done the new year's eve murder, that Big Ben is now after him for some reason, and this cell phone is somehow important, that Big Ben wants it, but you don't know why.'

'That's about it I suppose,' said Paul-Frank. 'What do you think?'

'It's a story and a half for sure,' said Max. 'But it sounds a bit vague to me. Tenny-rate, what are you going to do?'

'Asking you, aren't I,' said Paul-Frank. 'What do *you* think I should do?'

Max stood up. Paul-Frank did too.

'We better get going,' said Max.

'But, mate, what do you think I should do?'

Max shrugged, and indicated with his head and his eyes across the canteen to a man sitting alone at a window table. Paul-Frank followed his gaze.

'You could tell Aunty about your suspicions,' said Max quietly. 'Your intuition.'

'Who's Aunty?'

'I told you about him,' said Max. 'Aunty Glante. He's a top cop in CIB. Over there. Officer in charge of the Welly Alley Strangler case.'

They stood together at the table. Looking.

'You should tell him,' said Max again. 'Tell Aunty. I'll introduce you.'

'No way,' said Paul-Frank.

'Why not?'

'Got nothing to tell,' said Paul-Frank. 'Not yet anyway. What Ponytail told me wasn't much. All in my own head. A feeling.'

Max shrugged. 'Well, there he is,' he said. 'He's not here often so now's your chance.'

'No way,' said Paul-Frank again. Nervously.

'Well, no harm in meeting him anyway,' said Max. 'Come on. He's alright.'

And so Paul-Frank followed his partner across the canteen, edging and sidling their way between tables and chairs, occupied and otherwise, until they stood together at Detective Inspector Glante's table by a window.

'Aunty,' said Max to Detective Inspector Glante.

The policeman looked up from his lunch. 'Oh, g'day, Max. How the hell are you?' He seemed pleased to have someone to talk to.

'I'm good, mate. You?'

'I'm alright given the crap I'm going through today,' said Glante. 'Defence arseholes give me the shits. Who's this anyway?' he added looking up at big Paul-Frank.

'This is my new partner, Paul-Frank Ratanui,' said Max. 'Reecie's retired.'

'I heard that,' said the seated Glante who put down his filled roll and wiped his hand quickly on his suit coat before shaking hands with the standing Paul-Frank. 'I've seen you around, mate,' he said. 'Can't miss you actually. Know who you are. You were at The Lake before.'

He picked up his filled roll and took another bite.

'What are you doing here today?' asked Max.

'Sit down. Sit down,' said the detective through a mouthful of filled roll filling. Max and Paul-Frank pulled out a chair each opposite the lunching detective who added: 'Witness, Maxie boy,' said Glante, flicking out flecks of hard-boiled egg and lettuce in the saying. 'In the number two. Bloody awful business. But aren't they all.'

'Nothing to do with the Welly Alley Strangler is it?' asked Max tentatively.

Glante suddenly stopped eating and looked at Max intensely, suspiciously, for a moment – a brief moment – before relaxing again. He finished his filled roll and wiped his mouth and chin with a paper serviette before replying. 'Shee-hit no. That's bloody miles off,' he said quietly before loudly sucking air through his teeth as a means of clearing them of food debris. Then he picked up a Coke and drank it directly from the bottle. He put the empty bottle down, burped rudely and loudly, and patted his upper chest by way of explanation and apology. Then he looked across at Max Bridlington suspiciously again, his head to one side, and asked: 'Have you heard something, Maxie?'

'No,' said Max quickly.

Glante shifted his direct gaze across to Paul-Frank.

'You?'

Paul-Frank shrugged and shook his head quickly. Defensively. For some reason the old detective inspector made him feel guilty.

'If you heard anything around the court, in the cells, gossip, anything like that, you boys would tell me wouldn't you?' said the frowning detective with a hint of threat.

'Of course we would, Aunty,' said Max.

The detective looked again directly at Paul-Frank with his questioning hairy eyebrows now raised high. Paul-Frank suddenly felt guilty again. And intimidated.

'Course we would, Mr Glante,' he said. 'I definitely would.'

'Call me Aunty,' said a quickly-relaxed Detective Inspector Glante as he pushed back his chair. 'Bloody ridiculous I know but everybody does.'

Evidently Glante had finished his lunch and his conversation with the two security guards. He stood up, brushing crumbs and other food scraps from his shiny tie. 'Meeting before resumption with our QC,' he said. 'Such a *bitch.*'

Paul-Frank and Max pushed back their chairs and stood up.

'Good to meet you, Pauly,' said Glante. He took Paul-Frank's big hand across the table, shook it once, and was gone.

Paul-Frank and Max stood and watched the stooped figure in the unbelievably baggy suit walk through the canteen, coughing lightly and nodding to people on the left and right, until he went through the swing doors and out of the canteen.

'How does he know people call me Pauly?' stammered Paul-Frank.

'Aunty knows everything,' said Max. 'Absolutely everyone and every *thing*. Believe me.'

Chapter 14

Later that day – in fact it was early evening – Tatts McIndoe and Eric the Limp were sitting together in an almost empty pub on the waterfront. On a warm Wednesday afternoon, immediately after the summer holidays, this Irish pub, in a downtown business area, should have been busy, as other pubs were, with thirsty and gossiping civil servants on their way home from work. But The Battle of the Boyne was an old and run-down establishment in an old and run-down back street of abandoned and derelict waterside warehouses awaiting demolition and development and was thus not popular with any but an underclass of petty criminals in which the brothers, being still young, were new entrants.

They removed their jackets and draped them over a chair at a corner table before Tatts McIndoe bought a jug of cheap beer at the bar and took it to the table where the seated Eric the Limp was waiting. The shorter brother poured two foamy glasses before he sat down. The brothers were nervous and tense, spooked by their encounter with Big Ben – by his anger, by his throat-cutting gesture, by his putative instructions to kill Simple Simon and Ponytail, and especially by what he had almost revealed about himself in his blindingly angry outburst – about which the brothers had not spoken since they left Te Whareherehere on the bus. Only now, in the seclusion of this shabby and almost empty bar, did the shorter of the two dare to speak.

'You know he did them, Limpy, eh' he said plainly as he sat down. 'He must have.'

Eric the Limp picked up his glass and took a long draught. He wiped his lips with the back of his wrist before replying.

'Big Ben you mean? All them prozzie murders?'

'Exactly what I mean, my brother.'

'He must of,' said Eric the Limp. 'I figured that out all by myself.'

'I hoped you might. But I was scared you might say something stupid.'

'No way,' said Eric the Limp. 'I might be stupider than I look but in the mood he was in. I've never seen him like that before, Tatts. Never.'

'No,' said Tatts McIndoe. 'Neither have I. It was ugly.'

'I thought he was into drugs and blackmail and protection and hijacking fags and booze trucks and ramming ATMs. Harmless shit like that,' said Eric the Limp. 'Not murder. Not strangling prozzies.'

'Those poor girls,' said Tatts McIndoe as he took a long drink.

'Do you think he knows?'

'Knows what?' said Tatts McIndoe. 'That we know?'

'Yeah,' said Eric the Limp. 'Does he know that we know that he's him, the Welly Alley Strangler.'

'Hush your mouth,' said Tatts McIndoe anxiously.

'No farts are here,' said Eric the Limp.

'The walls have ears,' said his brother quietly.

'Do they?' said Eric the Limp looking nervously around at the smoke-stained and peeling walls.

Tatts McIndoe rolled his eyes in frustration.

'It's a metaphor, brother,' he said.

'Eh? What's a metaphor?'

Tatts McIndoe resisted the temptation. 'The walls don't have real ears, Limpy,' he said patiently. 'It's a figure of speech.'

'Oh,' said Eric the Limp. 'One of *them*.' He took one more suspicious look at the adjacent and dirty wall at his shoulder before taking another drink, emptying his glass.

Tatts McIndoe refilled both glasses.

'Oh, ta, Tatts,' said a very subdued and thoughtful Eric the Limp. And then, after a pause, he looked across the table deeply into his brother's eyes and said sombrely: 'You know, Tatts, I know I'm a bit of a shit fart and done some bad stuff — we both have haven't we — but not that. Not murder. I don't like murder. And I don't like what Big Ben done to them prozzies. And then he made us give that money to Simple Simon to do in another prozzie altogether. Farting hell, Tatts, there aint no way I'm going to do nothing bad to Simple Simon or that little Ponytail O'Gorman fart just to please Big Ben. No way José.'

It was perhaps the longest speech Tatts McIndoe had ever heard from his unloquacious brother. 'So are you thinking what I'm thinking, my brother?' he asked.

'Don't know what you're thinking, do I,' said Eric the Limp. 'But I'll tell you what *I'm* thinking, Tatts.'

'What?'

'I'm thinking that if we don't get that farting phone back, and if we don't get Simple Simon and Ponytail to shut up, and if Big Ben figures out that we know he's the Welly Alley Strangler, then he'll get one of his gang to kill *us* — me and you — to stop us from squealing and that.'

And that was the second-longest speech Tatts McIndoe had ever heard from his brother; fear stimulates garrulity in even the most taciturn people of limited vocabulary.

'I realize that, brother of mine,' said Tatts McIndoe in an attempt at soothing his brother's nerves as he soothed his own. 'But, listen: who's he going to get to murder us?'

'One of his gang of course,' said Eric the Limp.

'But, Limpy,' pleaded Tatts McIndoe, 'all his gang are locked up with him in The Lake. Or up in Parry.'

'Oh, yeah,' said a suddenly relieved Eric the Limp.

'All except two,' added Tatts McIndoe ominously.

'There you go, then,' said Eric the Limp, suddenly afraid and despondent again. 'We're rooted aint we.'

'No we're not, you idiot,' said Tatts McIndoe.

'Why not?'

'Because the two people in his gang who are *not* locked up is--' and instead of saying actual real names Tatts McIndoe simply pointed his index finger across the table at his brother before turning it around and poking it into his own chest '–and we're not going to murder ourselves are we.'

At which Eric the Limp slapped the table top with the flat of his hand and announced loudly: 'Brilliant. I'm getting another jug.'

'And then we're going to figure out how to find Simple Simon and Ponytail and tell them what we know,' said Tatts McIndoe.

'And warn them about Big Ben's murdering gang,' added Eric the Limp.

'You bloody idiot,' said Tatts McIndoe but not unkindly.

Chapter 15

'Can we sit inside tonight?'

'It's pretty warm,' said Max Bridlington. 'Wouldn't you rather sit in the garden bar?'

'Can't fit my bum into those dinky little chairs,' said Paul-Frank.

Which is why on that Friday after work — two days after their lunch-time encounter with Detective Inspector Glante in the court canteen — the two men were not outside in the cool-but-crowded garden bar but inside in the dim, stuffy and almost-empty public bar of *The Scales of Justice*. As always on a Friday night they had changed from their uniform into light and comfortable casual-wear. Max was anxious to get his end-of-week cold beer while Paul-Frank was anxious to speak to Max on a matter confidential. Not being able to sit comfortably in the garden bar's tiny chairs was partly his excuse to sit somewhere less crowded where their conversation could not easily be overheard by the legal types for whom *The Scales* was their watering hole of choice.

'Okay, you find somewhere comfortable to sit, Pauly,' said Max. 'I'll get us a jug.'

In a dark and quiet corner, beside a tall bookshelf stacked with dusty law books and an old lamp giving out a weak yellow light through its parchment shade, Paul-Frank found a low wooden table set with two wide shiny-leather armchairs. He sat down and waited. He didn't have to wait long but it was long enough to reflect again on his problem and to arrange his confused thoughts in a logical and sensible order. He was aware that Max — wise, kind and patient old Max, already a mentor and confidant after just two weeks — sometimes found his conversations rambly and disconnected. So in seeking Max's advice on this occasion he wanted to be clear and precise.

He took his phone from his shirt pocket and again called up the voice message.

'Oh, stink, Mr R. It's me, eh. I need to talk to you and I get this and I had to pay for the call,' said the breathless, frightened voice of Ponytail O'Gorman who hadn't paid for the call at all but had hijacked the Burger King payphone as usual. *'It's urgent as stink, eh. Come down to the shed at seven tonight.'*

Jeez, thought Paul-Frank, he's still sleeping in the shed. And seven tonight. Friday night of all nights.

He put the phone back in his pocket, annoyed that his evening with Max might be shortened by Ponytail's desire for a shed rendezvous. And then Max arrived with a jug of cold beer and two chilled glasses. He set the trio on the low table, sat down in the broad shiny-leather armchair opposite Paul-Frank, filled the two glasses, picked up one of them and held it forward towards his fretful companion.

'Cheers, Pauly,' he said. 'I've been waiting all week for this.'

'Cheers,' said Paul-Frank without enthusiasm.

They both took a drink, Max's longer than Paul-Frank's, and put down their glasses.

'Don't you drink during the week?' asked Paul-Frank.

'Nope,' said Max. 'Never have. I enjoy a beer, no doubt about it, but I enjoy it more when I have it less. Tenny-rate, Friday night, after work, before the weekend, has always seemed right to me.'

'Always done it like that?'

'I've been drinking here every Friday night after work, except holidays, for a bit more than fifteen years. Not on my own, mind. With old Wilf Reece, my partner before you. Every Friday night. And he started the tradition with his partner before me so it's a long tradition here at The Scales.' Max took another draught, put down his glass, and said: 'Tenny-rate, mate, is something bothering you? Something on your mind again? I get the feeling.'

Paul-Frank took another quick drink and leaned forward. 'Yeah,' he said. 'Really need to ask you something.'

Max rested back in the big chair. Relaxed. 'Ask away, young fellow.'

'Got a message—' Paul-Frank tapped his shirt pocket with his right hand '—on my phone, from Ponytail.'

'Ah! The bloke in your shed, right?'

'That's him,' said Paul-Frank. 'Wants to meet me tonight. In my shed again. At seven he says. Actually I think he's sleeping there most nights.'

'Why?'

'Well he's hiding isn't he,' said Paul-Frank. 'Like I told you. From Big Ben's boys.'

'No. I mean why does he want to meet you again?'

'Don't know,' said Paul-Frank. 'Says it's urgent. But I doubt it.'

'Are you going?'

'What do *you* think? That's what I wanted to ask you.'

'Personally I wouldn't have a bar of it,' said Max. 'Steer well clear I say.'

'But he'll be in my shed,' said Paul-Frank. He checked his watch. 'He's probably there already, waiting,' he added.

'Let him wait. What can he do?' said Max refilling both their glasses. 'Tenny-rate, have another beer, mate, and forget about him.'

'You reckon?'

'Absolutely. What can he do? You've got a good job, a prestige job, working for Courts and Corrections in the number one permanent criminal court in the great capital city of New Zealand. And he's a common old crook. A con man. Not even a successful one. You don't want to get mixed up with people like that, Pauly. I'd forget him. Just relax, eh. Friday night. Weekend ahead. Just relax.'

And so Paul-Frank Ratanui tried to relax; tried to enjoy his beer; tried to enjoy the company of his colleague and new friend Max Bridlington. But all the time he was thinking; worrying about Ponytail.

And what if Faith sees him there, he thought. Then what?

Chapter 16

Faith was in a happy jaunty humour when she left the bank to walk home on that sunny Friday afternoon at the end of January. The fact that Paul-Frank worked only Monday to Friday, with no shift work, and would be home all weekend, and every weekend, was still an exciting novelty.

This bright and positive mood carried her along Coutts Street – humming a little tune to herself, her handbag swinging at her side – and was with her as she turned right into Ross Street and took the short walk up to the house and in the gate.

Can't wait for the weekend, she thought as she walked cheerfully down the side of the house and around to the back door. Just me and Pauly, she thought. The whole weekend to do, well, nothing, but to do it together, that's the important thing, she thought. To be together doing nothing, with no commitments, for an entire weekend.

That at least was her expectation.

But her happy mood evaporated when she saw – she clearly saw, without doubt, no question about it this time – a figure moving behind the ragged curtain which covered the dirty dusty little window of Paul-Frank's decrepit shed. But evidently the said shadowy moving figure had spied her just as she had spied it. And now: nothing.

She didn't know exactly what she had seen but she knew she had seen something – a person – and was not now to be fooled by its absence. How dare you spoil my mood, my happiness, my pleasant thoughts about sharing the coming weekend with Pauly, she thought as she marched down the narrow concrete path leading to the rotary clothesline and then past the ancient persimmon tree and the white outdoor furniture, across the lawn to the shed at the end of the short back yard where she stood at the door, small but defiant and unafraid.

She saw that the padlock was locked in place but nevertheless she tried the door, rattled it by its large splintery wooden handle, more from frustration than expectation.

'Come out, whoever you are,' she said loudly; boldly
Nothing.

'I saw you,' she called. 'I know you're there. So come out.'
Nothing.

'I know you didn't get in this door but you must have got in somehow so you better come out the same way. Now.'
Nothing.

'Right!' she said angrily. She opened her wide and deep handbag and, head down, groped around in its depth feeling for her phone. 'Come out at once or I'll call the police,' she called, her head still down in the urgent and frustrating search for her phone.

She found it at last. By feel. And when she drew it from the deep dark depths of her bag, and turned it around, and up the right way, and readied herself to press out one-one-one, she was suddenly aware of a thin and small human figure – no taller than she, smaller even – standing at her side, silent and unmoving.

She jumped. Her heart raced. She brought the hand holding the phone up to her breast.

'Oh my god,' she said with fright. 'You gave me such a fright.'

'Oh, stink. Sorry, Mrs R,' said Ponytail, for that of course was the figure that was in and was now out of the shed and at her side.

'Who the hell are you?' snapped Faith. Although she had been afraid of who or what was in the shed, and had received a fright when she suddenly found a tiny old man, no taller than she, smaller even, at her side — as a result of her threat to call the police — she now didn't find the presence of the mild, short and narrow little fellow with a broad and toothy smile and a greying and silly-looking ponytail at the back of his balding head to be at all threatening. Indeed, he seemed absolutely inoffensive, almost amiable, like a cheeky little sprite. And so she added more gently: 'And what do you want?'

'You *are* Mrs Ratanui, eh,' said Ponytail with a smile.

'Yes. And you're Ponytail,' said Faith.

'Oh, stink. How do you know that?'

'Pauly described you very well. And your ponytail.'

Ponytail looked astonished. 'You call him *Pauly*?'

Faith raised her eyebrows, smiled and nodded.

'Foo,' said Ponytail. 'Wish I knew that in The Lake, eh. Would have been choice to know that.'

'You got stabbed,' said Faith bluntly.

Ponytail put his right hand, flat, to his right side below the ribs, bent forward slightly and winced theatrically. 'Hurt like stink, eh,' he said. He looked up to see Faith's reaction — seeking sympathy — but none was forthcoming.

Faith merely said: 'How did you get in and out of the shed so easily?'

'Back window's never locked,' said a now upright and unpained Ponytail.

'Oh,' said a surprised Faith. She thought Paul-Frank would be surprised too. 'Anyway, what are you doing in Pauly's shed?' she asked. 'What do you want?'

'I need Pauly's help,' said Ponytail with a cheeky grin and raised eyebrows.

'Mr Ratanui to you,' said Faith sternly.

'Yes. Mr Ratanui,' said Ponytail seriously. 'Mr R I call him. I need his help.'

'What help?'

'Bout the phone,' said Ponytail.

'What phone?'

'Totally right, Mrs R. Truth is it's disappeared, eh. Gone.'

'What?'

'S'gone. Completely disappeared off the face of the whole stinkin earth.'

'What *are* you talking about?'

'Stink, Mrs R. I tried to explain it to Mr R but he wouldn't listen. Totally refused. Wouldn't open his fat ears for nothing.'

'I can't say I blame him,' said Faith.

'But it's important. Lives at are stake.'

'Really?'

'True. Cross my heart hope to die if I tell a stinkin lie etcetera. He can help but he won't listen.'

'Can't anybody else help?'

'Nobody I can trust, eh.'

'So what's it all about?' asked Faith, giving Ponytail the invitation he needed; the opening which Paul-Frank had refused to consider.

'It's like this,' said Ponytail holding up his right forefinger to mark the start of a story. 'The Widow Partridge had my cell phone I gave her when she visited me in the infirmary to get it out of The Lake and her job was to post it to Mr R for safe keeping but she never done it she sent it somewhere else and she won't tell me where dunno why. Says it's safe but that doesn't help me cause the fellahs who want it are totally out to get me that's Tatts and Limpy. They're in Big Ben's gang, eh. See. It's a stinkin big worry but Mr R can protect me, eh, like he did in The Lake only screw who did only screw who cared about fellahs like me. But stink, Mrs R, he won't listen.'

'Hang on,' said a confused Faith. 'First of all, what about the Widow Partridge?'

'That doesn't matter now, eh,' said Ponytail. 'It's the stinkin phone that matters now.'

'A cell phone?' said a puzzled Faith. 'Posted to Pauly here?'

'No!' insisted Ponytail. 'That's what *s'posed* to have happened, eh, but she stinkin posted it somewhere else and she won't tell me where.'

'Why?'

'She says it's better if I don't know.'

'Why?'

'Cause if I don't know I can't tell.'

'But who would you tell?'

'Big Ben's boys of course,' said Ponytail. 'Tatts and Limpy. They'd do anything to get that stinkin phone.'

Of course nothing that Ponytail said made any sense to Faith.

'And what's so special about this phone?' she asked.

'Lips are totally sealed,' said Ponytail with a lip-zipping gesture. 'But Big Ben wants it and'll do any stinkin rotten thing to get it if you know what I mean.'

'No I don't,' said Faith.

'Don't what?'

'Know what you mean, I mean,' said Faith. 'I don't know what you're talking about,'

'Doesn't matter,' said Ponytail.

'So what do you want Pauly to do?'

'Well he knows Big Ben doesn't he,' said Ponytail. 'In The Lake.'

'But don't you know?' said Faith. 'Pauly doesn't work in The Lake anymore.'

'I know *that*,' said Ponytail. 'But he could still stop them boys, eh. From beating me up I mean. Murdering me even if you know what I mean.'

'What boys?'

'Tolja,' said Ponytail impatiently. 'Tatts McIndoe and Eric the Limp. They beat up the Widow Partridge already.'

Faith was truly shocked. 'The Widow Partridge got beaten up?'

'Well to tell you the absolute honest truth they didn't beat her up zactly but they made a mess of her place. Gave her a big scare if you know what I mean. Wanting to know where the stinkin phone is.'

'Come on, Ponytail,' said a puzzled and annoyed Faith. 'What's this all about? Really?'

'Foo, don't know if I want to tell everything to a nice lady like you.'

'Tell me,' said Faith. She still had her own cell phone in her hand and she rocked it threateningly in Ponytail's face.

'Stink, Mrs R. It's about the Welly Alley Strangler if you really want to know. You know about him?'

'Yes,' said Faith tentatively. She didn't like the sound of this and could perhaps see why Paul-Frank was so reluctant to get involved.

'Well, there's me, and Big Ben Pye, Eric the Limp, Tatts McIndoe, the Widow Partridge, Simple Simon and Aunty Glante and Mr R of course, and all them five dead prozzies,' said Ponytail quickly.

'Six, actually. Six innocent young women, Ponytail,' said Faith angrily. 'Six innocent young women who did nothing to deserve what was done to them by that evil man.'

'Totally right, Mrs R, of course,' said Ponytail quickly bending and bowing slightly by way of an apology. 'But Simple Simon never done it – the last one or none of them – and Big Ben's trying to make Aunty think he done it but he never never did and the proof's in the pudding which is in the phone that the Widow Partridge was supposed to have posted to Mr R but didn't and now everyone wants that phone and no one knows where it is sept the Widow Partridge.' Ponytail looked plain frightened when he looked helplessly at Faith. 'I'm in a real stink now,' he added pleadingly. 'A real deep stink if you know what I mean.'

At that point the little man grimaced, glanced at his watch and looked up the yard to the back door and the kitchen window beside it and then back to Faith.

'When will Mr R be home?' he asked, tapping the face of his watch. 'He's supposed to meet me at seven o'clock.'

'Have you been in touch with Pauly?'

Ponytail nodded.

He looked so frightened, so little and pathetic, that Faith couldn't help pitying him.

'But he's at the pub,' she said. 'Friday night. With a colleague. For ages. I don't think he'll be back by seven.'

'But I left a message on his phone to meet me here at seven.'

'I don't think he's going to drop everything on your say-so,' said Faith.

'Oh, what a stinkin mess,' said Ponytail despairingly.

'Come on then,' said Faith kindly, sympathetically. 'Come inside and tell *me* all about it, eh?'

'Oh, stink, Mrs R,' said a meek and unresisting Ponytail. 'I can't do that, eh. What would he say about getting his old lady involved?'

'Come on,' insisted Faith.

And so little Ponytail O'Gorman followed little Faith Ratanui up the back yard, across the lawn, under the large and ancient persimmon tree, past the white outdoor furniture, past the rotary clothes line, up the narrow path to the house and eventually into her little kitchen where he sat meekly at the kitchen table — where Paul-Frank and Faith shared their breakfast each morning and their dinner each evening — and waited and watched as Faith made them both a simple Friday-night tea of fried bacon and eggs, black pudding and tomatoes with buttery white toast, followed by hot and milky tea, which they consumed together. Ponytail appreciated the meal. Better than Burger King all the time, he thought. And it was while they were eating, or more accurately when they had finished eating and were enjoying their big mugs of hot and milky tea, that Faith quizzed Ponytail about his reasons for hiding in Paul-Frank's shed and the big deal about the cell phone. And when it was over, when Ponytail had told Faith about the photo of the Widow Partridge and Simple Simon on new year's eve which proved Simple Simon couldn't have committed the new year's eve murder even though Big Ben had paid him money in advance to do it, and otherwise about as much as dared about the whole affair — but not about stabbing himself to get to the prison infirmary and so escape from Big Ben and his gang so he could get the phone back to the Widow Partridge, and not about the other secret thing on the phone —

Faith asked him what he was going to do; where he was going to go.

'Mr R's not going to meet me at seven is he,' said Ponytail in response, looking at his watch.

'No,' said Faith. 'He has a drink with his colleague on Friday nights. He could be quite late.'

Ponytail looked worried. He looked at his watch again.

'So what are you going to do now?' asked Faith.

'I'm sorry Mrs R that I've been sleeping in your shed,' said Ponytail. 'Even though Mr R said I couldn't. But Big Ben's boys would never look for me there.'

'Where else could you go?'

'Only to the Widow Partridge – she wants to marry me you know – but they'll still be watching her place for stinkin sure if you know what I mean.'

'Well you can't hide in our shed any more and that's that,' said Faith, emphatically, and Ponytail could see that business was what she meant. 'It's not even hygienic,' she added. 'And there's a rat.'

'Stink, no!' said a horrified Ponytail.

'That's what Pauly said.'

'I'm definitely outa there,' said Ponytail. 'But, stink, Mrs R, what can I do? Where can I go?'

Thus he pleaded with pathos sufficient to induce Faith Ratanui to furnish him with funds sufficient to pay for a motel room for two weeks or more.

'And get some new jeans and a clean t-shirt,' she said. 'The Kilbirnie Red Cross shop will be open tomorrow. On the corner. You know it?'

'I know it,' said Ponytail.

And thus did Faith Ratanui become the latest of many women to donate money to the Ponytail O'Gorman charity fund.

'Oh, thanks heaps, eh,' said Ponytail. 'I'll pay you back for sure totally, eh. Cross my heart and hope to die etcetera.'

'We'll see,' said a sceptical Faith.

'And you'll see if you can get Mr R to help? Please? I've gotta find the phone. And I've gotta find Simple Simon.'

'I'll see what I can do,' said Faith. 'Now go, before Pauly gets home and finds you here. I'll talk to him in my own way about everything you told me.'

'Pauly,' said Ponytail with a wicked giggle. 'I wish I knew *that* when I was in The Lake.'

And then he was away into the darkling evening by taxi – ordered and paid for by Faith – to the nearby Crescent Motel which Faith had booked in his name: Mr Patrick O'Gorman.

Chapter 17

Faith was waiting.

'Why didn't you tell me?'

She was annoyed rather than angry.

Paul-Frank, towering over his annoyed little wife, shrugged his thick and heavy shoulders in much the same way and for much the same reason that a guilty little boy, confronted by an accusing and knowing mother, substitutes an evasive shrug for an oral answer.

'That's not an answer, Paul-Frank Ratanui,' said Faith in a sharp motherly fashion.

They were standing in the gloomy kitchen. It was dark outside. The remains of Faith and Ponytail's fried tea were congealing on the plates which were still on the table.

'But what about my tea?' whimpered Paul-Frank.

'I'll make your tea when I'm good and ready, man,' said Faith. 'Not before.'

'When will that be?' plainted Paul-Frank. 'I'm so blimmin hungry, Fay.'

'When we've finished talking about this,' said a determined Faith.

'But–' said Paul-Frank pointing at the two plates on the table.

'I had tea with your friend in the shed.'

'Eh?'

'Ponytail.'

'Ponytail was here? In our house.' Paul-Frank was truly shocked. 'You cooked him tea?'

'Yes. And he told me everything.'

'He did?' Paul-Frank was now surprised as well as shocked. '*Everything?*'

'Yes,' said Faith doubtfully. 'Well, as far as I could tell everything. At least allowing for the fact that he's a crook, a con man and a pathological liar, I think everything. At least I got the gist of it.' After a pregnant pause she added: 'I think.'

'But–'

'Now, Pauly,' interrupted Faith sounding less cross, 'You've got tell me what you know about this Ponytail business and what it's got to do with you.'

'Jeez, Fay,' protested Paul-Frank. 'Know nothing. Nothing to do with me at all.' He pointed timidly to the chair he was standing beside and asked meekly: 'Can I sit down, love?'

Faith nodded sternly and Paul-Frank sat down.

'Give me that,' said Faith kindly, pointing.

Paul-Frank handed her Ponytail's soiled plate; she carried it and hers to the sink.

'Now,' she said as she returned and sat down at the table. 'What's this all about with your pal Ponytail.'

'Oh, Fay,' said a distressed Paul-Frank. 'Not my pal.'

'He says you're friends.'

'Told you. Used to look out for him in The Lake,' said Paul-Frank. 'He's so little and old and harmless and he used to get picked on so I looked out for him. Part of my job in a way. But doesn't make him my pal? Does it?' he added hopefully.

'I don't know,' said Faith. 'But *he* thinks you're pals and he tried to post you a cell phone. Or at least that was the plan for his lady friend.'

'The Widow Partridge,' said Paul-Frank.

'You know about that? About the cell phone?'

'Don't know anything about it,' said Paul-Frank. 'But I know that's what he said.'

'And?'

'Not allowed a cell phone in The Lake,' said Paul-Frank lamely.

'Don't be naïve, Pauly,' said a not-naïve Faith.

'But how would he have got a cell phone?'

'I don't know. You worked there. How do cons do these things?'

'If I blimmin knew that—' said Paul-Frank.

'Well, he had a cell phone,' said Faith. 'He said he never talked on it — they don't you know — but they use it for texting. He used to get texts from the Widow Partridge. And he could tell her what was going on. Like a spy.'

'Must have been going on right under my blimmin nose,' said Paul-Frank. 'The little creep.'

'They're all doing it according to him,' said Faith. 'And now, thanks to the photo that the Widow Partridge sent him on the phone which he showed to Big Ben, Big Ben Pye knows that Ponytail's pal Simple Simon couldn't have done the new year's eve murder like he was supposed to,' said Faith knowingly.

'Eh? You know all that?'

'Yes,' said Faith bluntly. 'So?'

'But what photo?' asked a mystified Paul-Frank. 'And a murder? I thought so. But he told you all that?'

'He wanted to tell *you*,' said Faith.

'But what about this photo? And the murder?'

'The lady – the Widow Partridge – by the way, Pauly, you did tell me about her didn't you?'

'Yes. I told you. She's an official at The Lake. Ponytail's official. Rich old bird I think.'

'Yes. Well apparently someone took a photo of her and this man called Simple Simon on new year's eve. Maybe it was selfie. Anyway do you know him? Simple Simon?'

'Yeah,' said Paul-Frank. 'Know him sort of. Blimmin big bastard. My age. About. Handsome dude but not much furniture in the attic. Did some time, not much, in The Lake. Twice I think.'

'Well, it sounds strange doesn't it. Why would this Widow Partridge – I wonder what her real name is – why would she have a photo taken with this big dumb crook Simple Simon, a friend of Ponytail's, on new year's eve. Ponytail said there were lights and new year's eve bunting and a big *Happy New Year* sign in the background. A party.'

'So?' said Paul-Frank with a shrug. 'Jeez, love, I'm so blimmin hungry.'

'Wait on,' said Faith. 'Let me tell you this. It helps me figure it out for myself.'

'Take long?' asked Paul-Frank hungrily. 'And why do you care? I really don't care about blimmin Ponytail and them others.'

'You care about justice though, Pauly, don't you? Now listen. According to Ponytail this Simple Simon was supposed to have murdered some girl – any girl I think – on new year's eve and make it look like the work of the Welly Alley Strangler.'

'Oh my god, Ponytail told you this?'

'But he says that this horrible Big Ben Pye is the real Welly Alley Strangler and that he paid Simple Simon to do the new year's eve murder but that he did all the others. According to Ponytail he purposely got himself arrested so he'd be in The Lake when Simple Simon did the new year's eve murder. But he never actually did it.'

'Who never did it? What?'

'This Simple Simon never actually did the murder he was paid to do,' said Faith. 'That's according to Ponytail.'

'Still don't get it, love,' said Paul-Frank.

'Don't you? Look, if there's another murder exactly the same as all the others while Big Ben's in jail then the police would maybe think that if Big Ben didn't do that one maybe he didn't do all the others either. And maybe Ponytail's friend Simple Simon did them all.'

'Cops aren't that dumb,' said Paul-Frank. 'But what's the photo got to do with it?'

'Oh, Pauly, look. Somehow the Widow Partridge gets this new year's eve photo of her with Simple Simon on her phone and sends it to Ponytail in The Lake. I don't know why. Just to make him feel better on new year's eve. So he receives it on his cell phone see. And then he stupidly shows the photo around the place — showing off about the rich official visitor in the photo who wants to marry him — and Big Ben sees it and realizes that Simple Simon probably couldn't have done the murder on new year's eve that he was paid I don't know how much to do. Not if he's at a new year's eve party somewhere in the boo-eye.'

'Must have been Big Ben who stabbed Ponytail,' said Paul-Frank. 'Or one of his little savouries. Trying to get the phone with the photo. Oh, Fay, Big Ben is trouble with a capital trub.'

'But he didn't get it did he,' said Faith. 'Ponytail says he hid it and gave it to the Widow Partridge when she visited him in the infirmary. That's when he told her to post it to you.'

'But I didn't get it, did I.'

'No. Because Ponytail says she posted it somewhere else and she won't tell him where.'

'Why not?'

'He says that she says if he doesn't know where it is he can't tell anyone else.'

Paul-Frank shook his head. He was bewildered.

'See, the thing is, Pauly, if Ponytail can get hold of his phone with that photo on it he can prove to the police that Simple Simon couldn't possibly have committed that horrible new year's eve murder.'

'Must be more to it than that though,' said Paul-Frank. 'The photo must have been on the Widow Partridge's phone to start with. Before she sent it to him. Probably still is.'

'No,' said Faith. 'Ponytail said it's been deleted from her phone.'

'And now Big Ben wants it deleted from Ponytail's phone but his boys can't find it,' said Paul-Frank. 'Or him.'

'Or Simple Simon,' said Faith.

'Big Ben paid Simple Simon in advance,' said Paul-Frank. 'That's what you said isn't it?'

'That's what Ponytail said,' said Faith.

'Yeah, well Big Ben will be blimmin pissed off about that to start with,' said Paul-Frank. 'But hang on, love,' he added. 'If Ponytail's right and Simple Simon didn't do the new year's eve murder he was paid to do, then who the hell did?'

'I thought of that too,' said Faith. 'Which means the real Strangler could be still on the loose.'

'Or another strangler altogether which means Big Ben could still be in the frame for the first five murders,' said Paul-Frank.

'It's a mystery, Pauly,' said Faith. 'And your little mate Ponytail is stuck in the middle of it.'

'Love,' said a hungry and pleading Paul-Frank. 'He's *not* my mate. But why are you even thinking about all this? It's a blimmin mess. Why do *we* have to get involved?'

'We don't, obviously,' said Faith. 'But don't you feel sorry for Ponytail and Simple Simon?'

'For Ponytail I do,' said Paul-Frank. 'He's so hopeless and harmless. But Simple Simon? A dumb and stupid crook. His own fault for getting involved. Taking the money. Feel more sorry for me. Still haven't had my tea.'

'Oh, sorry, love,' said Faith getting up. 'I'll do it now. Me and Ponytail had bacon and eggs and black pudding, a fried tomato and toast. Will that be okay?'

And so, while Faith stood at the stove, cooking Paul-Frank's dinner, she continued talking over her shoulder about Ponytail's visit.

'Did you know that Big Ben sent two of his gang around to the Widow Partridge's to look for the phone?' she asked.

'No,' said a waiting Paul-Frank from his place at the table. 'When was that?'

'I don't know exactly,' said Faith. 'But they broke in and roughed up her place. And her a bit I think. According to Ponytail. That's when they deleted the photo from her phone.'

'Really?'

'Apparently she's got a flash apartment in Oriental Bay. She's pretty rich according to Ponytail.'

'Which is probably why he tried to con her and ended up in The Lake in the first place.'

Faith set a plate and cutlery in front of her hungry husband, together with salt and pepper and a bottle of HP sauce, and began serving his dinner from the frying pan. She returned the hot frying pan to the kitchen bench and joined hungry Paul-Frank at the table.

'Delicious,' he said as he broke the soft yolk of a fried egg and swirled a piece of toast through the resulting gooey and golden mess. 'Who roughed her up anyway?' he asked as he ate.

'Ponytail knows who they are.'

'Be that Tatts McIndoe and his stupid brother Eric the Limp.'

'So who are they exactly?' asked Faith.

'Couple of stupid blimmin kids trying to impress Big Ben,' said Paul-Frank between mouthfuls. 'They used to visit him in The Lake. So they obviously didn't find it. The phone I mean.'

'No. She told them she didn't know who she posted it to,' said Faith. 'She told them she sent it to the address Ponytail gave her but she couldn't remember what it was. But she told Ponytail she posted it somewhere else altogether where they'll never find it.'

'And she won't tell him.'

'No.'

'Jeez, Fay, I wonder where she sent it?'

'Ponytail said he's got no idea,' said Faith.

'Won't stop them looking,' said Paul-Frank. 'They'll be looking for Ponytail right now you bet. And he's down in our shed the little creep.'

'No he's not,' said Faith.

'What do you mean, love?'

'I mean,' said Faith slowly, 'I booked a motel room for him and gave him enough money to survive for a couple of weeks at least. And get some decent clothes.'

'Oh, Jeez, love, a clever girl like you gave the notorious Ponytail O'Gorman money. How does he do it? Getting money out of women? Even *you*. So where's this motel?'

'I'm not telling you.'

'Why?'

'What you don't know can't hurt you,' said Faith with a smile.

'But what if Tatts and Limpy come round here looking for Ponytail?'

'Well, you honestly don't know where he is do you,' said Faith. 'And we have no idea where the phone is either do we.'

Paul-Frank finished his dinner. He pushed the plate back and sat back in his chair, fully satisfied.

'Really don't like this, Fay,' he said worriedly. 'It really is blimmin scary and weird.'

'Don't worry, Pauly,' said a remarkably calm Faith. 'I'm going to get to the bottom of it.'

'You? How? What can *you* do, Fay?'

'I can use the one thing I have that Ponytail and all those other stupid crooks don't have.'

'What's that, love?' asked a curious Paul-Frank of his clever little wife.

'Brains, Pauly,' she said. 'Brains.'

Chapter 18

They say you can't beat Wellington on a good day, and Saturday, the last Saturday of January that year, was one of those days you couldn't beat.

'A lovely day and another wonderful weekend together,' said Faith that morning. She was looking at the back garden, through the open kitchen window, at the unbeatable day; she was washing the breakfast dishes while Paul-Frank did the drying. She stopped for a moment, her hands – one of which was holding a dish-washing brush – poised over the hot and sudsy water. She looked at Paul-Frank. 'You know, Pauly, I really can't think why you worked in The Lake for so long,' she said.

'Neither can I,' said Paul-Frank.

'You know what I'm going to do? Later?' she asked somewhat mysteriously. 'This afternoon? And you too?'

'No, love.'

Faith casually resumed the washing up while Paul-Frank innocently continued his work with the tea towel.

'I'm going to ring up Ponytail, you're going to pick him up from his motel, and we're going to have a barbecue and give him a proper good feed.'

'Oh, love,' protested a dismayed Paul-Frank.

And so at four o'clock in the afternoon of that beautiful unbeatable Wellington day Paul-Frank Ratanui was obliged to sit at his garden table, under the large and ancient persimmon tree, with Ponytail O'Gorman, his erstwhile prisoner whom he had always pitied but never particularly liked and with whom Faith was now chatting away amiably as though she and he were the oldest and dearest of friends. He's an incorrigible crook, thought Paul-Frank. He's a sad little man with no friends who needs help, thought Faith. And I've got to cook him an expensive fillet steak and let him drink my Speights while I drink lemonade because I have to drive him back to his motel which by the way we are paying for, thought Paul-Frank. I'm going to help him find his phone and his friend Simple Simon, thought Faith. This is choice, thought a newly-scrubbed-clean-and-shaven Ponytail garbed in his new second-hand ensemble.

'I think you can start the barbie now, Pauly' said Faith. 'And I've made you a good nutritious salad to go with it,' she said to her thirsty and hungry guest.

'Choice, Mrs R,' said Ponytail, raising his bottle in grateful acknowledgement. 'I could murder a good feed, eh.'

'In a minute, love,' said Paul-Frank.

It was now Faith's intention to subject her plainly undernourished guest to a friendly quiz — the sound and smell of sizzling fillet steak and pork sausages serving as an incentive to talk — and so learn more about the missing cell phone business, about his friends Simple Simon and the Widow Partridge, about the two young thugs who had evidently roughed up the above widow (who sounded strange, eccentric, kind and rich, and who, for some unfathomable reason, wanted to marry the odd little con man), and what the whole affair had to do with the Welly Alley Strangler and the six girls so brutally murdered. But as she was about to start her interrogation the interrogatee – who was sitting contentedly, smugly, in his garden chair facing the house – suddenly looked, what? both horrified and terrified. He slammed down his half-full bottle of beer (causing it to fizz up and overflow onto the table), panickly pushed back his chair – its back legs caught in the soft surface of the lawn causing it to topple to the ground on its back – and stood up, his thin face blanched, a picture of dread and fear.

'Stinkin Jeez-*US!*' he said, his black eyes open wide and bulging.

Paul-Frank and Faith – who were sitting opposite the terrified old fellow, facing down the garden, their backs to the house – quickly turned around in fright to see what had so scared him; he who, in his panic, had stepped back two or three paces and so fell backwards over the fallen wooden garden chair where he now lay awkwardly, trapped and tangled in its unyielding arms and legs. They saw two men – familiar to us, familiar to Paul-Frank, well known to Ponytail, but unknown to Faith but by reputation – standing at the corner of the house looking across at the very suburban Kilbirnie scene of a Saturday evening backyard barbecue. And as Paul-Frank and Faith watched, and a frightened Ponytail struggled helplessly, futiley, to extricate himself from the arms and legs of the garden chair in whose hard and unloving embrace he was so awkwardly trapped, the two boyish young thugs swaggered arrogantly, threateningly, across the yard, crossing the narrow concrete path to the rotary clothesline in their progress, and stood on the lawn in front of the two people seated at the wooden garden table under the large and ancient persimmon tree. Ponytail, meanwhile, who had at last freed himself from the clutches of the heavy wooden chair, returned it to its standing position and crouched behind it looking fearfully, pathetically, over the top of its sheltering back.

Of course Faith immediately guessed the identity of the two uninvited guests firstly from Ponytail's reaction to their arrival and then from their appearance. They're not much more than boys, she thought. One was tall and thin with a thin and pimply face, the other short and somewhat overweight. They were both dressed incongruously in their tight black trousers, black vinyl jackets, black heeled boots and white open-neck shirts, and the tall one was wearing black sunglasses. They stood together, their hands in their trouser pockets, their legs apart, their heads set to one side with affected nonchalance. To any normal person they looked utterly ridiculous, standing there like that, dressed as they were, in a quiet Kilbirnie garden at the end of an unbeatable Wellington summer's day. And so Faith — being the most normal person there — laughed aloud. A split-second later Paul-Frank, being the second most normal person there, also laughed. But Ponytail, being not entirely normal at all, did not laugh but cringed back, whimpering, behind the dubious protection of his wooden chair.

'Pray, at what are you laughing at, Mrs R?' asked Tatts McIndoe meekly.

'Yeah, waddya laughing at?' said Eric the Limp aggressively.

All the same, he removed his sunglasses with a flourish, as if he knew that they were contributing to Faith's amusement, folded them ceremoniously, and slipped them into the pocket of his jacket. But even without the sunglasses he had to look at the trio from the corners of his eyes due to the angle at which he had purposely and rigidly set his head.

'It's them,' said a cringing Ponytail from behind his wooden chair. 'Limpy and Tatts. Big Ben must of stinkin sent them.'

Tatts McIndoe held out both his hands, palms down, and waved them flatly from left to right to left in a calming gesture that Faith and Paul-Frank took to signal: no, we come in peace. It was an implication missed entirely by the nervous Ponytail.

'Wadda you boys doing here?' he cried. 'Waddya stinkin want? Don't hurt me.'

While at first taken aback by the surprise appearance of the two alleged thugs in his back yard on a fine and quiet Saturday evening at the end of January, just as he was going to get the expensive fillet steaks and less expensive but still potentially delicious pork sausages onto the barbecue, Paul-Frank quickly found their presence and appearance to be annoying, patently ridiculous, and not the slightest bit threatening or intimidating. Indeed he thought they looked like white and weedy undernourished characters from a cheap black-and-white B-grade gangster movie. And so he slowly, carefully, pushed back his chair and stood up to exhibit his great height and bulk to the two thin and pasty-faced young pretenders.

'Who the hell are you?' he asked threateningly although it was an entirely rhetorical question – he knew very well who they were – while, given his nature, his posture was an entirely empty threat.

But the two visitors were not to know that; they suddenly looked shocked, taken aback, frighted. As a result they each took a quick backward step and so caught the heels of their boots on the edge of the narrow concrete path and tripped back awkwardly. And while Eric the Limp quickly recovered his balance Tatts McIndoe fell completely backwards landing heavily on his ample backside. He recovered himself eventually, standing up with his brother's help while brushing at the tight bottom of his trousers with both hands; they then stood together, side by side on the narrow concrete path leading to the rotary clothesline, blushing with embarrassment.

Blushing. Limpy and Tatts blushing. Ponytail couldn't believe his bulging black eyes. For the first time in weeks he began to relax. Indeed, he quite enjoyed the sight of his two feared enemies – agents of the even more feared Big Ben Pye – looking so ill-at-ease and embarrassed and not at all scary. Obviously Mr R scares them without even trying, he thought. Just as I thought he would, he thought. And with so much tension released he couldn't suppress a high giggle. And such was his confidence that he left his position crouched behind his chair and crept around the front to sit on it, at least on its front edge, with a cocky and smug coolness; with Paul-Frank frightening the boys so easily, and their obvious blushing embarrassment at tripping and looking so foolish, he was now looking forward to what might happen next.

But what happened next surprised Ponytail as much as it surprised the visitors' involuntary hosts. Because suddenly they, the two black-suited young visitors, abandoned their preposterous posturing as if even *they* knew they looked ridiculous. They took a step forward together off the narrow concrete path over which they had only moment ago tumbled so inelegantly, and stood, a little ill-at-ease in the manner of young men all over the world, at the high pitch of awkward late adolescence, dealing with their tumbling hormones, and looked shamefacedly at Paul-Frank, willing themselves to do what they now found so difficult: to answer his question.

'So, who the hell *are* you?' asked Paul-Frank again.

At last Tatts McIndoe found his voice: 'Desmond Ypres McIndoe at your service,' he said pronouncing the name of the Belgian town and its namesake battle after both of which he was named: Wipers. He followed his announcement with a ceremonial bow.

'Eric Saint Elvis Baxendale if you must know,' said Eric the Limp sullenly at which serious announcement Ponytail laughed out loud and received an empty glare from the speaker.

'I thought yous were brothers,' said Ponytail whose fear of the two men had by now evaporated entirely.

'We are,' said Tatts McIndoe. 'But I had a different father.'

'And I had a different mother,' said Eric the Limp.

Faith smiled a slight, knowing and sympathetic smile and said kindly, gently: 'Come and sit down, you two idiots,' at which invitation the newly-arrived not-quite brothers visibly relaxed, sighed, and sheepishly dragged out two of the heavy garden chairs to join the party at one end of the heavy wooden outdoor table under the large and ancient persimmon tree laden with unripe fruit.

'Now what do you boys actually want?' asked Faith with a pleasant smile. 'Have you come to beat up Ponytail?'

'Fay!' said a shocked Paul-Frank.

'Oh, Mrs R,' squealed Ponytail whose terror returned with the mention of the potential of physical violence against his small, frail, vulnerable and cowardly person. 'Don't joke about it.'

'Don't be stupid, Ponytail,' said Faith to a still cowering, whimpering Ponytail. 'Relax will you. These two young blokes aren't here to beat you up. Do you think they'd arrive here like this, in broad daylight, if they had any evil intentions? They want something.' And then turning to the brothers she asked plainly: 'Now, boys, why are you here? What is it you want?'

'You tell her,' said Eric the Limp to his brother.

'What? Now? Just like that?'

'Fart, yeah,' said Eric the Limp. And then to Faith he said: 'It's a bit embarrassing to tell you the truth.'

And so Tatts McIndoe looked up, into the canopy of the large and ancient persimmon tree laden with unripe fruit, as if looking for heavenly guidance and strength. He and his brother then leaned forward onto the table to confide in the other three who leaned forward ready to listen; he then took a deep sighing breath before speaking. And when he had finished, only a few moments later, the two Ratanuis and one O'Gorman were themselves speechless.

Chapter 19

'The thing is, Mrs R,' began Tatts McIndoe.

'Call me Faith,' said Faith.

'Oh. I see. Well, the thing is, Faith, my brother Eric and I want to ask your husband, Mr Ratanui there, for his help and protection.'

'What!' shouted Paul-Frank.

'Shut up, Pauly,' said Faith, at which pet name revelation the brothers looked at each other and smiled.

'Yeah, it's Pauly, eh,' said Ponytail knowingly to the brothers as if they were now his best friends.

'Go on, Desmond,' continued Faith, ignoring Ponytail; her use of Tatts McIndoe's real name caused the brothers to smile again.

'Please call me Tatts, Faith,' said Tatts McIndoe. 'Everybody does. Not Desmond.'

'And call me Limpy,' said Eric the Limp.

'Okay, Tatts. Limpy. Now what were you saying?'

'The fact is that Limpy and I are sick of Big Ben ordering us around from prison,' said Tatts McIndoe. 'Furthermore we don't approve at all of what he did. Indeed, we don't like it one bit.'

'What exactly did he do?' asked Faith.

'For one thing he beat up that big bouncer to get himself into The Lake on purpose,' said Eric the Limp.

This was news to Paul-Frank whose wide-eyed expression revealed his surprise.

'On purpose? Why'd he do that?' asked an equally-surprised Faith.

'Then he made us give Simple Simon two-and-a-half grand to kill that last girl,' said Tatts McIndoe. 'On new year's eve.'

'The mysterious girl?' said Faith. 'They don't even know who she is.'

'He never done it,' protested Ponytail across the table. Loudly.

'We never knew what the money was for,' pleaded Eric the Limp. 'Honest, Faith. We thought it was just a drug deal or something harmless like that.'

'But why'd he do that?' asked Faith again, again ignoring Ponytail's interruption.

'And he promised him another two-and-a-half biggies when the job was finished,' added Eric the Limp.

'Really? Why?'

Despite the unpleasant nature of the gradually unfolding story Faith found it fascinating. Paul-Frank didn't.

'To put off the long arm,' said Tatts McIndoe. 'To make them think that maybe it was Simple Simon who was the Welly Alley Strangler.'

'He wanted Simple Simon to take the rap for killing all them prozzies see,' interrupted Eric the Limp.

At this point Ponytail stood up in protest. 'But Simon never done it,' he said again, as loudly and vehemently as he could. 'I stinkin totally know for sure he never done it ever.'

'We know that too, Ponytail,' said Tatts McIndoe.

'Everybody bloody knows that, you dickhead,' said Eric the Limp crudely.

'Limpy!' said Tatts McIndoe indignantly. 'Language.'

'Oh, yeah, sorry Mrs R, I mean Faith,' said Eric the Limp. 'Sorry for saying bloody and dickhead and that. But the photo in the phone.'

'Stink, you guys,' said the standing Ponytail to the sitting brothers while Paul-Frank and Faith sat back and observed, listened. 'It's not just that. I know totally for sure that Simon never done the new year's eve one or none of them.'

'So?' said Tatts McIndoe.

'Doncha get it?' said Ponytail. 'It's why Big Ben is after me. Why he sent yous to the Widow Partridge's. Why he's so desperate to get my phone.'

'Why?' asked the listening quartet.

'Are yous stinkin stupid or what?' asked Ponytail rhetorically. 'Because Big Ben done in all them prozzies. Because Big Ben's the Welly Alley Strangler.'

Paul-Frank and Faith said nothing but the other two, the two who had discovered the same thing for themselves in their own way, and had been so revolted by the knowledge, said together: 'Is that all? We know *that*.'

'You do?' said a surprised and deflated Ponytail.

'But hang on,' said Faith. 'If you three know that Big Ben's the real Strangler then how come the police don't know? And how come they don't do something about it?'

'We know,' said Eric the Limp, 'because we figured it out all by ourselves. But the long arm, well they're dumb aren't they.'

'And if they do know — and they might to be fair — they need proof don't they,' added Tatts McIndoe.

'But—' interrupted Ponytail.

But Faith interrupted his interruption: 'Wait on, Ponytail,' she said. 'Let's hear what Tatts has to say first.'

'But—' interrupted Ponytail again.

'Wait!' insisted Faith with uncharacteristic impatience. 'Go on,' she said to Tatts McIndoe.

'Well, that's it isn't it,' he said. 'The long arm think that Simple Simon strangled that girl on new year's eve and we know he didn't. And they think that maybe he did all the others as well so they're after him but—'

'But he's disa-bloody-peared,' interrupted Eric the Limp. 'And with us after him, on Big Ben's orders, *and* the long arm, I don't bloody-well blame him. Sorry.'

'But what I don't understand,' said Faith, ignoring both the swearing and the apology, 'is that if you say you *know* that Simple Simon didn't – couldn't – do the new year's eve murder because of the photo that the Widow Partridge sent to Ponytail—'

At this point in Faith's declamation Ponytail let out a loud sigh of obvious frustration.

'—and that Big Ben couldn't have done it because he was locked up in The Lake—'

'Stink, Mrs R,' said an increasingly distressed Ponytail.

'—then who on earth murdered that poor mysterious, friendless, nameless girl on new year's eve?'

'The truth of the matter is that we simply don't know about that,' said Tatts McIndoe. 'But we know that Simple Simon didn't do it and we're pretty sure that Big Ben did all the others – the first five – and that he's the Welly Alley Strangler.'

At which point Paul-Frank leaned forward and spoke for the first time: 'But where's the proof?' he asked momentously.

And then the still standing, still frustrated Ponytail pushed back his chair and virtually shouted: 'I'm trying to stinkin tell you all. I *had* the proof, I really did. Big Ben's actual stinkin totally real confession, recorded on my phone which has gone missing. I've got to find that phone.'

'I see,' said Faith thoughtfully. 'A recorded confession. Well, we really *do* have to find that phone then, don't we. Wherever it is.'

'The Widow Partridge,' said Ponytail.

'Tried that,' said Tatts McIndoe.

'Well, we'll try again,' said Faith. And then, turning to Ponytail, she asked: 'Where does she live?'

'I don't know,' said a suddenly thoughtful Ponytail who now wondered why he didn't know the address of the woman he always said wanted to marry him.

'I do,' said Tatts McIndoe.

'So do I,' said Eric the Limp.

'So you do,' said Faith.

Meanwhile, in the back garden of a handsome brick-and-tile two-storied steeply-roofed house in far-away Martinborough – surrounded by many hectares of grape vines bearing their slowly-ripening berries – the custodians of Ponytail O'Gorman's little black cell phone were themselves relaxing after their own Saturday evening barbecue, sharing a seven-year-old bottle of the old estate's own *pinot noir*.

PART II

Chapter 20

When, in eighteen-ninety-eight, the young William James Faridale – newly-arrived from County Wicklow – bought his land at Waihenga, on the southern fringe of the newly-established township of Martinborough, he was hopeful, optimistic even, that it would soon become a productive sheep farm and that he and the family he intended to raise there would together, through determination, persistence and hard work based on his deeply-held faith, eventually pass on to his descendants a sound and prosperous agricultural business and so found a Martinborough and Wairarapa farming dynasty. But like many settlers of the time his naïve optimism was in vain; he discovered only later, when it was too late, that his land on what was to become Dry River Road was underlaid by an ancient bed of river shingle and was thus dry and unproductive. Nevertheless, undeterred, the young Faridale persisted in his efforts until eventually he was able to make a passable living from mutton and wool sufficient to marry and begin raising a family.

Hard-working and earnest, he was not without a native good nature and a pleasing Irish humour, and so easily made many friends in the district including the older and locally influential

William Beetham. From him he learned that Beetham's French wife had successfully grown the *pinot noir* grapes of her homeland and had even exhibited her *vin de Nouvelle-Zélande* in Paris with notable success. He also learned from Beetham that conditions on his farm and Beetham's, as well as on land to the west and east of Martinborough, were almost identical to those in Burgundy. As in that famous but faraway French region Beetham's vines grew slowly and struggled to fruit but in the process produced a low yield of berries of an intense and concentrated flavour.

And so, with Beetham's help and advice, large swathes of Faridale land were planted out with *pinot noir* cuttings imported especially from France. Growth was slow and the vines peculiarly unproductive but Faridale accepted the advice of the experienced Beetham and tended his vines patiently more as a hobby than with expectations of profit.

And then in nineteen-hundred-and-eight – when he was just thirty-two years old and his son Thomas William was a two-year-old infant – fanatical agents of the temperance movement swept through the Wairarapa tearing up grape vines and destroying anything connected with the growing, harvesting, brewing, fermenting, distilling, storing, distribution and selling of any form of alcoholic liqueur. The Beethams were compelled to submit and so watched helplessly as the crazed prohibitionists gleefully ripped their precious vines from the ground and burned them in the very middle of the vineyard adjacent to their homestead and small winery.

But young William Faridale was not to be intimidated by a gang of obsessive and misguided hoodlums; indeed he obtained an injunction against the members of the temperance movement so bent on destruction – in which he was supported by the local and sympathetic constabulary – and successfully argued his case in court. His argument was that the little amount of juice he was able to obtain from his young vines was so sour that it could be made into nothing better than vinegar for use in sauces, pickles and chutneys. Indeed, to prove his point he presented the court magistrate with a glass of the cloudy and unpalatable pink juice, freshly pressed. Having sipped tentatively at the sour stuff the ancient and somewhat pompous colonial official – utterly untutored in the origins of old-world grape varietals and the finer points of winemaking, his red and bulbous nose glowing proof of his propensity for a nightly pint of porter– readily agreed that the liquid pressed from William Faridale's grapes could never be turned into a palatable wine and so, ruled His Honour, the vines could be left in the ground to grow and mature and provide the fruit whose extracted juice appeared to be ideally suited to the manufacture of a quality vinegar of which the growing town of Martinborough would one day be duly proud.

But long before His Honour announced his ruling the temperance militants lost patience with the legal process and so moved on leaving the Faridale farm's vines rooted safely in their stony ground. And so over the years, under the adult management of William's heir Thomas William Faridale, followed by *his* son Thomas Simon Faridale, the long rows of *pinot noir* vines, planted into the gravels of Dry River Road, forever stunted and struggling, were added to, quietly and without announcement or fuss, until they covered the whole of what was once the large and unproductive Faridale sheep farm. Of course in time others came to recognize the district's unique *terroir* and so brought their own cuttings of other French varietals, growing and producing small quantities of some of the world's finest cool-climate wines, especially the *pinot noir* for which Martinborough is now so famous and which grows in no greater abundance on vines which have been reaching deep into the gravels of Dry River Road for more than a hundred years.

Set deep in this by-now vast Faridale vineyard – its prizewinning *pinot noir* wines known around the world by its famous black and yellow label of *'Faridale Farms, Wines of Martinborough, New Zealand, Founded 1898'* – were two identical brick-and-tile two-storied steeply-roofed homesteads each on its own hectare of lawn, each at the end of its own long and intentionally-curving drive, each separated from its neighbour by at least five hundred metres, and both shielded from the road by a long row of aged and ragged macrocarpa trees backed by a shelter-belt of thick native bush. Furthermore, they were unidentifiable by either gate or letterbox; the postman and local tradesmen knew the addresses, knew the owners personally, but a stranger would pass unaware of the narrow and unkempt entrances and drives or of the substantial houses which stood in quiet dignity at their terminuses.

And it was in the back garden one of these hidden homesteads – the one farther from the town – that the so-sought-after so-called Simple Simon sat nonchalantly in the Saturday evening sun with his beautiful and new young friend Lucy Dixon with whom he had, only that day, after almost a month of being together holed up in the Martinborough house, come to an agreement about their shared future.

'So how long's it been now?' asked Simon who here, now, in this place, looked and sounded anything but simple.

'I got here on Christmas day,' said Lucy. 'Wellington I mean.'

'I remember,' said Simon. 'And you never hear from anyone in Liverpool?'

'No.'

'No one? Not ever?'

They had, at the beginning, agreed to never have this conversation; but the passage of time, the charm of the cottage garden in which they sat, and the vineyard which surrounded them, the scent of heritage roses in the warm evening air, the romance which was now palpable between them, and perhaps a little too much of the estate's own prize-winning wine, had combined to relax them both and loosen the tongues which had been necessarily tied by caution when they were thrown together by circumstances forced upon them by their work and their superior officer.

'Never,' said Lucy. 'Never will. Not ever. That's the arrangement.' She took a sip of wine. 'This is proper lovely wine isn't it,' she added.

'Best in the world,' said Simon. 'But won't you miss them? Your colleagues and friends and that?'

'I told you, Simon, didn't I,' said Lucy. 'There's nobody there. This is my life now, see.'

'It's sad though, isn't it,' said Simon. 'You being an orphan.'

'It's all I've ever known.'

'But no parents. No brothers and sisters. No uncles or aunts or cousins or anything.'

'You don't miss what you never had, darling,' said Lucy. 'But let's not talk about that. It's such a lovely evening. And you're so lucky to live here.'

'I don't live here, Luce,' said Simon. 'Used to. When I was a kid. But not for years.'

'But *we'll* live here won't we like?' asked Lucy. 'More wine please?'

She held out her empty glass; Simon reached down for the bottle which sat on the lawn beside him and refilled both their glasses.

'Not here, darling,' said Simon. 'Not here exactly. Although it'll be mine one day I suppose.'

'I know that,' said Lucy. 'But–'

'I'm not really interested in the business, Luce,' said Simon. 'Viticulture. Winemaking. All that. I'm a cop.'

'Me too, love,' said Lucy. 'But–'

'Don't worry,' said Simon reassuringly. 'After this Uncle Aunty promised to get us a placement together somewhere around here. Together. There's lots of small stations in the Wairarapa. Traffic jobs too.'

'I can't wait like,' said Lucy with a smile.

'Back in uniform in a small-town station, eh,' said Simon. 'The country life for us.'

'It'll be dead lovely all right,' said Lucy. And then, looking across at her new fiancé – although there had been no official announcement, no ring, not yet – she asked with a puzzled look: 'Do you *have* to call him that?'

'Who? What?'

'Uncle Aunty? Its sounds right stupid. Uncle Aunty.'

'I've always called him that,' said Simon. 'He's my uncle.'

'What's his real name? Not Aunty.'

'Tim,' said Simon. 'But no one ever calls him that. Except mum. And Aunty Pansy.'

'I call him DI Glante,' said Lucy. 'I have to. And sir.'

'So do I,' said Simon. 'At work.'

'I've got him to thank for this,' said Lucy, holding up her glass. 'For meeting you and that.'

'I'm glad,' said Simon. 'But what happened? You can tell me now.'

'Well, thanks to him I never met anyone in Wellington like I was supposed to.'

'You were going to be a beat cop weren't you? In Wellington?'

'That was the plan,' said Lucy. 'But he intercepted me. With the commissioner's approval he said. Right in the lobby at the main entrance in Victoria Street.'

'And?'

' "I've got a special job for you, young lady," he said,' said Lucy, trying unsuccessfully to adopt a New Zealand accent in a low register. 'You know what he's like, right mean and gruff sounding. "Just one special assignment before you don the official uniform of a proud New Zealand WPC. Just one undercover job. And it starts now." '

'And that was that?'

'Exactly.'

'Well, we'll both be back in uniform soon,' said Simon. 'No more pretending.'

'I agree.'

'And you know, acting dumb all the time is *really* hard. I'm glad it's all over to tell you the truth.'

'Me too,' said Lucy.

'But, Luce, one more thing. Your real name?'

'Lucy *is* my real name.'

'You know what I mean,' said Simon teasingly.

'I'm not supposed to,' said Lucy. 'Ever.'

'What? Never?'

'Perhaps when we married,' said Lucy. 'Perhaps.'

Chapter 21

Detective Inspector Tim Glante hated early mornings. He always had. He hated late nights too. And always had. He had always longed for regular hours: eight hours a day, five days a week. But as a member of the New Zealand Police he had never had regular hours. Shift work, weekend work, they were only to be expected at the beginning of a police career; but now, as a Detective Inspector in CIB, near the end of his career, he often thought he was entitled to regular hours.

'Be alright if I was a desk jockey,' he used to say to Pansy, his wife.

'You'd hate to be a desk cop,' was her consistent response; she knew how much he despised policemen who finished their careers as pen-pushing administrators.

'I know,' admitted Glante who these days was sometimes stimulated by but more often despondent about the nature of his work in CIB.

Now, on this Sunday morning – not especially early but a Sunday, his day of rest – he was especially despondent; despondent about his work; despondent, disappointed and disillusioned about the case of the Welly Alley Strangler. And annoyed with himself that his conscience and dedication were driving him to rise early on this Sunday – the first opportunity he had had to get away in a week of professional commitments and yet a day which should have been one of rest – to start a journey which he hoped but was not entirely sure would contribute to closing one of the most awful and frustrating murder cases of his career in the criminal investigation branch.

'I don't know *exactly* when I'll be back, love,' he said to his wife. 'But I *will* be back tonight. So don't worry.'

After so many years of marriage Pansy Glante still willingly, happily, got up early when necessary – even on a Sunday – to ensure her Tim started his day with at least some toast and a cup of his favourite sweet black tea. And after so many years of marriage she knew enough not to ask questions of her policeman husband so she merely said: 'Be careful, Timmy,' as she nodded kindly, smilingly, and offered her cheek for a goodbye kiss.

'You do know where I'm going don't you?' he asked.

'No,' replied his wife. 'Of course not.'

'I'm going up to see Simon at the house,' he said in a stage whisper. 'First chance I've had all week.'

Pansy's eyes and mouth opened wide in an involuntary expression of surprise and understanding. 'Oh,' she said as he pecked at her proffered cheek before leaving the house.

Outside the old detective went slowly, almost reluctantly, to his car, which was standing in the open carport. Once seated at the wheel he sat for a few moments, quietly, thinking, staring ahead through the windscreen at the ragged hedge which needed trimming, but seeing nothing, and said, aloud, while thumping the top of the steering wheel with the heel of his hands: 'Jesus, I'm too old for this.'

Although he and Pansy were wealthy – far wealthier than your average detective inspector near the end of his career should be – thanks to Pansy's inheritance, Tim Glante preferred to live quietly and without ostentation in suburban anonymity. Accordingly, he and his wife still lived in the unpretentious and now somewhat shabby Hataitai bungalow they had bought not long after their marriage. And, in keeping with his preference for ordinariness, he had recently chosen the small, inexpensive, second-hand faded-red little Toyota in which he now sat, depressed and dejected. Now, after one deep sigh of resignation, he started the car, turned painfully to look over his left shoulder as he backed into the street, and set off down a quiet Waipapa Road for the village and thence through the Mount Victoria tunnel for the tiresome drive over the notorious Rimutakas to Martinborough; a drive of a little more than an hour in the light traffic of an early Sunday morning. He hoped that once he had safely secured the object of his journey he would have a little leisure time there in Martinborough – some therapy time to relax in the peace of tranquillity of the countryside he loved – before returning to Wellington later that day. He knew he would be returning either in utter disappointment, to the comfort of home and the soothing companionship of his wife, or flushed with success to Central where the clever young scientist Rembrandt Hawxwell and his staff would be waiting ready to work through the night.

How the day ended depended on what if anything he found on the little cell phone which even now, on this early Sunday morning, was still sitting harmlessly – turned off – on the kitchen counter of the two-storied brick and tile homestead in Dry River Road on the fringe of Martinborough.

The two residents therein were just rising.

Chapter 22

'What do you want?'

The housekeeper could see the image of two boys – faces she didn't recognize – on the bright security screen. She was instantly and instinctively suspicious; protective of her mistress, her property and her privacy. The boys on the screen, standing on the pavement on the street far below, could hear her but not see her. They looked puzzled, stupidly seeking the source of the voice.

'Eh?' said Tatts McIndoe.

'You pressed the buzzer,' said the housekeeper. 'Waddya want?'

'Who are you?' asked Tatts McIndoe.

'You mind your own damn business, boy,' said the housekeeper.

'But isn't this the Widow Partridge's place?' asked Tatts McIndoe.

'So what?' asked the housekeeper in reply. 'And she's *Mrs* Partridge to you, eh.'

'Mrs Partridge. Right. We want to speak to her. Mrs Partridge. Is she there please?'

'Not here,' said the housekeeper.

'Where is she?'

'Away.'

'Away where?' asked Tatts McIndoe tactlessly.

'None of your business, boy,' said the housekeeper predictably. 'Who do you think you are anyway? You wanna leave a message?'

'No message. But who are *you*?' asked Tatts McIndoe rudely. 'What are *you* doing there?'

'I'm Mrs Partridge's housekeeper,' said the housekeeper indignantly.

'But you weren't there last Sunday,' said Tatts McIndoe. Foolishly.

'I don't usually work on Sundays, boy,' said the housekeeper. 'Who do think I am?' And then, suddenly she added: 'Oh, so you're the two. All the broken glass I had to—'

At that, and at a signal from Faith who was standing to the side of the camera, Paul-Frank stepped behind the brothers, gripped them by their collars, one in each fist, and hauled them away from the concealed security camera lens which was adjacent to the building directory. Faith stepped forward.

'I'm really sorry to trouble you,' said Faith, standing on her toes to reach up to the intercom. 'But it's really important that we speak to Mrs Partridge.'

'She's not here,' said the housekeeper abruptly; she didn't recognize Faith's voice and so squinted at the screen to see if she could recognize the face. She didn't.

'Do you know where she is? Will she be back soon?'

'Yes and don't know,' said the housekeeper; she was not inclined to be cooperative. Indeed, her instructions were to not disclose her mistress's whereabouts to anyone, especially not to strangers.

'Oh, dear,' said Faith, and the housekeeper saw the worried look on her face and watched as she turned to someone off camera on her right and heard her ask: 'What on earth are we going to do now?'

And then the housekeeper – who in fact was rather intrigued by this encounter with the strange group of people safely distant in the street far below – saw in the screen the top of a familiar balding head with thin grey hair gathered together and pulled back tight.

'Is that you, Patsy O'Gorman?'

'Who's that?'

'It's Hinemoa, cuz. Tolaga Bay, eh.'

'Ae! Tena koe, Hine.'

'Kia ora, Patsy. Mrs P said you were in the hōhipera.'

'I was, Hine. I stinkin was. But I'm alright now. Sweet as, eh.'

'Oh, that's so nice, boy. But what do you want?'

'I want Rosie,' said Ponytail. 'But what are you doing here, Hine?'

'I'm her housekeeper,' said the housekeeper. 'Been for ages, eh.'

'I never knew that,' said Ponytail. 'So is she there, Hine? I need to speak to her real bad. Urgent as stink, eh.'

'Oh, I don't know,' said a worried and doubtful Hinemoa. 'Those people with you. I don't know.'

'They're ka pai, Hine. Oku hoa,' said Ponytail with as much reassurance as he could manage with Faith urging him on at his side.

'What did he say?' she whispered to Paul-Frank.

'He said we're okay. We're good. We're his friends,' whispered Paul-Frank in reply.

And so Faith prodded Ponytail in the side and nodded her enthusiastic approval of his line of persuasion while Tatts

McIndoe and Eric the Limp stood silently well out of range of the camera.

'Quit it,' said Ponytail, pulling away in response to the prod.

'What's that, Patsy?' asked the worried housekeeper.

'No, nothing, Hine. But can you *please* tell me where Rosie is? It's urgent important as stink.'

'But she said—'

'But she'd want to see *me* now that I'm out of the hospital, Hine, eh. Don't you reckon?'

'Oh, I don't know,' said the housekeeper, worried and doubtful.

'She wouldn't like it if she knew I wanted to see her and you turned me away like if you know what I mean?'

'Oh, Patsy, cuz, you make me so confused, eh. I don't what to think.'

'What I think you think is you think you should tell me as long as I don't tell no one else, eh. Cross my heart hope to die etcetera.'

'That's *right*, Patsy,' said the housekeeper, somewhat relived. 'You mustn't tell nobody else.' But then she added doubtfully: 'But what if—'

'If you get in for trouble, Hine, I'll explain everything to Rosie to make it all right again,' said Ponytail.

'Really?'

'Totally promise,' said Ponytail.

'Oh, alright then,' said the housekeeper. 'As long as you keep it a big secret between us.'

'Cross my heart and hope to die etcetera,' said Ponytail.

At which the housekeeper Hine leaned into the intercom and imparted the following vital information in a whisper: 'She's gone to the big house.'

Despite the whisper it was information that was easily heard by the other four standing in the sun on Oriental Parade that Sunday morning, the last day of January, to the side of their little ponytailed companion, well clear of the camera lens. But while they received the half-dozen simple words from the housekeeper loud and clear, they, the words, comprised and conveyed information that meant nothing to them. Importantly, though, they could see that the information did mean something to Ponytail.

'I see,' he said slowly, adding: 'You know why?'

'No!' said the housekeeper indignantly. 'Course not.'

'You know when she's coming back?'

'No!' said the housekeeper again, loudly this time. She stepped back from the intercom and looked at it suspiciously; at the little image of the top of Ponytail's head. 'She often goes up there,' she added. 'You know that. She doesn't have to tell me why.'

'Okay, Hine,' said Ponytail calmingly. 'Okay. Okay. Everything's okay. But why are you working on a stinkin Sunday?'

'Mrs P said if I work today I can have tomorrow off. Me and Willy are going to the pictures.'

'Willy's here too?'

'Of course,' said the housekeeper.

'Foo,' said Ponytail wondering what Hinemoa's thieving brother Willy — they were his cousins on his mother's side — was doing in Wellington. 'Anyway, Hine, thanks heaps, eh.'

'I hope it's alright I told you,' said the now-having-second-thoughts housekeeper.

'It's ka pai,' said Ponytail. 'Hei konā rā, Hine, Ka kite ano.'

'Haere rā, Patsy,' said the housekeeper as she switched off the intercom with a slow and worried shaking of her head. 'Ka kite--' she added to the blank screen. 'I hope not.'

Chapter 23

'So what was that all about?' asked Faith.

The five of them were sitting in Paul-Frank's Land Cruiser on a quiet Oriental Parade opposite the Widow Partridge's apartment building. Paul-Frank was in the driver's seat, Faith was in the passenger seat, while Ponytail sat in the back looking tiny between his two enemies-turned-allies who each had a back window seat. Faith had to twist around awkwardly to speak to Ponytail.

'She's got a big house in the Wairarapa,' replied Ponytail.

'Whereabouts in the Wairarapa?'

'Martinborough.'

'Makes sense,' said Tatts McIndoe. 'The party and that.'

'How come she has a big house up there when she has a big flash apartment over there?' asked Faith pointing to the Widow Partridge's apartment building across the street.

'I dunno, Mrs R,' said Ponytail. 'That's what stinkin rich people do, eh.'

'Which is why she became one of your marks,' said Paul-Frank to the windscreen.

'Oh, stink, don't be like that, Mr R,' protested Ponytail to the back of Paul-Frank's shaven head. 'We're gonna get married when all this is over and done with if you know what I mean.'

'Doubt it,' said Paul-Frank sceptically.

'Don't worry about that now,' said Faith impatiently. 'If we want to find the phone we have to find Mrs Partridge. Which means we have to go to this house of hers in Martinborough. That's probably where she posted it anyway.'

'I should've stinkin thought of that for myself,' said Ponytail.

'Agreed,' said Tatts McIndoe. 'Let's go there.'

'Kin oath,' said Eric the Limp who was looking forward to a long ride in Paul-Frank's big Land Cruiser.

'Jeez. Want to go *now*?' asked Paul-Frank of his little wife who seemed to have taken charge of the project.

'Yes, Pauly, of course,' she answered as if there were any doubt.

'Martinborough,' said Paul-Frank as he leaned forward to start the car. 'Where in Martinborough?'

The big diesel roared into life and waited tickingly.

'Do you know where this house is?' asked Faith over her right shoulder.

Ponytail merely shook his head slowly but Faith didn't see.

'Eh?' she asked .

'I said no,' said Ponytail.

'No idea?' asked Faith.

'Something to do with a vineyard,' said Ponytail vaguely.

'So you've never been there?'

Ponytail shook his head slowly again.

'Eh?' called Faith.

'I said no,' said Ponytail again.

'A vineyard you say?'

Ponytail nodded his head.

'Eh?'

'I said yes,' said Ponytail.

'Do you know which vineyard?' asked Faith. 'A name?'

'Lots of vineyards in Martinborough,' said Paul-Frank. 'Let's get going.'

And so Paul-Frank turned the Land Cruiser out onto Oriental Parade, made a U-turn, and headed the big vehicle back to town where he could join the motorway north heading for State Highway Two.

'Stink, Mrs R,' said Ponytail. 'So many questions, eh.'

'You've never been there?' asked Faith again.

Ponytail shook his head slowly again.

'Eh?'

'No!' Ponytail almost shouted the response. Almost angrily.

'You've never heard Mrs Partridge talk about her house in Martinborough? A street name or something? Anything?'

Ponytail shook his head slowly again. 'Fraid not, Mrs R,' he said. 'Sorry.'

Despite not knowing his exact destination Paul-Frank enjoyed the drive north. In fact he enjoyed driving – he always had – and he especially enjoyed driving his big, roomy and powerful Land Cruiser. He and Faith rarely travelled far from home, and even more rarely carried passengers in the back, and so he took quiet pleasure from giving his passengers a comfortable ride imagining how impressed they would be with the great Toyota power over which he had complete control, and with his smooth accelerating, braking and cornering, especially as they made their winding way up and then down through the bush- and forest-wilderness of the Rimutakas.

But the passengers in question – or rather the brothers – were at first hardly aware of anything but the novelty of the journey. They had not only never been in such a nice big and powerful car but they had never been out of Wellington. Deprived by their origins and upbringing their world had been bounded to the south by Cook Strait; and they had never been farther north than Porirua and the Queensgate Mall in Lower Hutt. Now, for the first time in their lives, they found themselves in the unfamiliar semi-rural streets of Upper Hutt. And then, before long, they were climbing to the frighteningly great heights of the notorious Rimutaka range on frighteningly winding roads that were frighteningly narrow cut from hills that were frighteningly steep falling into valleys that were frighteningly deep. And as well as being astonished by the dramatic Rimutaka landscape around them – the like of which the brothers had never, could never have, imagined – they were equally astonished by what they didn't see, what in fact was *not* there to be seen: for the entire length, in duration and distance, of the ascent and descent of the Rimutakas they saw no villages or towns, no houses or shops, dairies or pubs, no buildings of any sort, no footpaths, no power lines or street lamps, no animals, and no people except those few fellow car travellers with whom they shared the road on that quiet Sunday morning.

When at last they left the Rimutaka road – and they were each silently grateful that Paul-Frank had successfully negotiated its myriad hazards – they passed through quaint Featherston, the smallest town the boys had ever seen, before entering the lush green dairy country on State Highway Fifty-three on their way at last to Martinborough.

As a result of so much variety of scenery, both dramatically mountainous and tranquilly pastoral, the young city-slicker brothers, overwhelmed by all they had seen and were seeing, said nothing for the entire duration of the journey; not that they would have had anything meaningful to say. Rather, like children to whom every sight and every experience is excitingly new, they merely stared wide-eyed out their respective windows. Indeed, the whole experience of the trip to Martinborough was making them feel insignificant and unimportant. In fact, since the shock of recognizing Big Ben's deeply dastardly and murderous character, their showy confidence – never anything more than a pathetic act of adolescent bravado – had continued to shrink until it was now moribund and would soon be entirely extinguished. For years to come they would remember their strutting immature cockiness with painful embarrassment.

Meanwhile Ponytail couldn't believe he was sitting between them, the two heartless young thugs who had been so nasty to the Widow Partridge and who had so intimidated him by their very existence. Because of his own sense of inadequacy – realizing now that he knew so little about the Widow Partridge – he didn't realize that the brothers were now utterly overwhelmed by the apparent vastness of the open and empty countryside around them. But he, whose origins lay in the remote East Coast, was neither moved nor impressed by a bush-covered mountainous wilderness, nor by quaint villages or green and open spaces populated by countless ungulates, large and small. Rather, he sat quietly, unimpressed, between the quiet and amazed young brothers, looking sullenly at the road coming towards him between the two front seats. And thinking. He was torn between being grateful that he now had both Mr and Mrs Ratanui on his side, helping him find his phone and so prove Simple Simon's innocence – Mrs R leading the search for his phone and Mr R providing the protection he had always wanted – and being resentful that Mrs R expected him to know the exact location of the Widow Partridge's Martinborough home which knowledge he acknowledged he should indeed possess. The fact was, he knew now – although he was reluctant to admit it — that he knew very little about the Widow Partridge. For a start when asked he hadn't even known where in Wellington she lived; even the stupid young brothers Tatts McIndoe and Eric the Limp had been able to find out that for themselves. Nor had he realized quite how very rich she really was; rich enough to have a luxurious penthouse apartment on expensive Oriental Parade, and to have a housekeeper (who turned out to be his own cousin Hinemoa); why, he wondered, didn't I know these things? He felt humiliated that she, the Widow Partridge, wouldn't tell him where she had posted his phone and that he had been too stupid to figure it out for himself: her house in Martinborough. And although he had heard her speak of the Martinborough house he felt dumb for not knowing anything about it including exactly where it was. Nor did he know anything about a vineyard. He remembered Simple Simon saying something about a vineyard when they were in The Lake together; if only he had been more curious; if only he taken more notice; if only he could remember now what Simple Simon had said then. And why and how, he wondered now, suddenly, did Simple Simon know stuff about the Widow Partridge that he didn't know? And why, he wondered further and for the first time, was Simon celebrating with her on new year's eve when that picture was taken? I can't believe how stinkin dumb you are, he said to himself. But I hope Simple Simon's alright, he thought, wherever he is.

'The pub,' said Paul-Frank pointing to the beautiful old Martinborough Hotel on the corner on his right.

They had arrived at the end of Kitchener Street, between Texas Street and Kansas Street, in the very centre of little Martinborough. They were forced by the one-way system to turn left into Memorial Square and so the others in the Land

Cruiser caught no more than a glimpse of the classical two-storied colonial wooden building with its distinctive covered veranda running the entire length of both its street frontages. But a glimpse of the hotel was all Ponytail O'Gorman needed. His sullen mood evaporated; he suddenly unclipped his seat belt, turned and kneeled on the back seat, his arms hooked over the back, staring out the rear window, like an excited child, at the Martinborough Hotel.

'That's stinkin it!' he cried. 'Stop the car, Mr R. Stop the car.'

It wasn't hard to find a place to park on Martinborough's Memorial Square on a Sunday morning and so, without knowing the reason, Paul-Frank patiently pulled over and prepared to stop the Land Cruiser. But even before it was completely stopped and parked Ponytail had opened the door and clambered over the black-trousered long legs of Eric the Limp. Thus he was at Faith's lowered window as Paul-Frank killed the engine.

'What the blimmin–' said Paul-Frank to the little old face at Faith's open window .

'That's it,' said Ponytail excitedly; he was so jumping up and down with excitement that his ponytail was flying about in sympathy. 'That's stinkin it for sure.'

'Stop it, Ponytail!' shouted Faith through the open window. 'What is *it*? What are you talking about?'

Ponytail stopped his leaping about and thrust his head into the car while his skinny bottom end outside was still jigging about with excitement.

'That,' he said, pointing back to the hotel and shifting his glance between Faith and the hotel. 'That hotel. The veranda up there. That's where the photo was taken.'

The Martinborough Hotel. Tatts McIndoe and Eric the Limp each remembered their interview with the Widow

Partridge; they looked across the car at each other guiltily but said nothing.

'The photo of Mrs Partridge and Simple Simon?' asked Faith. 'The new year's eve photo? There.'

'Totally yes,' said Ponytail.

'Let's get out,' said Faith to the others in the car. 'Quick.'

Chapter 24

When they were all out – five obvious city-based strangers clustered together on Martinborough's Memorial Square late on a fine Sunday morning, the last Sunday of January – Faith said: 'I bet someone in the pub knows who Mrs Partridge is and where her house is.'

The public bar of the big Martinborough Hotel was not only small but was unlike the public bar of any pub that any of the five had ever seen.

'Stinkin posh, eh,' said Ponytail quietly, voicing only what the others were thinking.

There was a thin young man and a not-thin older woman serving behind the bar. They both looked up – indeed the entire population of the bar was looking at the five strange-looking city-type strangers – but it was the oldish biggish barmaid who said: 'G'day, folks. And what's it to be?'

And so of them all only Faith stepped up to the bar and quietly asked her question. It was a question that made the barmaid laugh out loud. And so she spoke out loud; not answering the question but addressing the entire bar of watching and listening patrons.

'They want to know if we know a Mrs Partridge,' she called with a laugh.

Her call was answered by hoots of good-humoured laughter. Faith and her companions cringed with embarrassment.

'I saw her in the car this morning,' called out someone from the far corner of the room as the laughter subsided. 'In Dublin Street.'

'Coming or going?' asked the barmaid loudly.

'Coming,' called the voice. 'Willy was driving.'

'Willy was driving?' said a puzzled Ponytail. 'Cousin Willy was driving?'

He was speaking, quietly, asking himself a question to which he didn't expect an answer. But even if he had spoken aloud he would not – could not – have been heard over the noise that surrounded him and his four companions.

And what an odd sight they were; five Wellingtonians standing together in that small and busy bar: big brown shaven-headed Paul-Frank Ratanui and his tiny white wife Faith; tall and skinny and pimply Eric the Limp and his short squat brother Tatts McIndoe dressed in their tight black trousers, black heeled boots and white open-neck shirts – they had at last dispensed with their vinyl jackets – and, of course, the smallest of them all, little Ponytail O'Gorman, old, grizzled, balding, with a long steely-grey ponytail falling down his back. Five ill-at-ease city-looking strangers standing together in the middle of the bar in a small provincial town while fifty-or-so drinking locals laughed with uncruel derision at their foolish almost unbelievable ignorance.

'But we don't know anything about wine, do we Pauly,' protested Faith when the good-natured old barmaid had explained the cause of the laughter.

Paul-Frank turned down his mouth and shook his big head slowly and seriously.

'We just *don't*,' she insisted as the other three members of the party joined Paul-Frank in his slow head-shaking.

'But, surely, Faridale wines,' said the barmaid. 'Everyone's heard of Faridale wines.'

'We haven't,' said Faith, looking at the others who all looked mystified and began shaking their heads again.

'But, lady, they're famous all over the world,' said the thin young man in a white apron who was wiping down the bar. 'Famous.'

'Sorry,' said Faith. 'Never heard of them.'

And so, when the locals had finished laughing, bored with the novelty of actually meeting five people at the same time in the same place – in Martinborough – who had never heard of the region's largest and most famous vineyard, a strange quintet indeed, the barmaid said to Faith: 'I'll show you a map.'

'Oh, dear, I don't get maps,' said Faith. 'Could you show my husband instead?'

'Course, love,' said the barmaid. 'Go around there,' she said to Paul-Frank indicating to her right. 'Into the library.'

Paul-Frank had to excuse himself numerous times as he edged and elbowed his way through the standing and sitting drinkers, who all patted him on the shoulder or broad back in friendly recognition, until he found himself in a small restaurant/dining room, its tables set for lunch with white linen tablecloths, fine silverware and crystal wine glasses. He could see the barmaid waiting for him in the library at the far end of the restaurant. When he finally joined her he found that she was standing beside a large and stylized map of Martinborough – an enlarged version of the map used by wine tourists to the town – which was framed and fixed to the wall. It showed the name and location of each of the region's vineyards and wineries.

When he was standing with her, close enough to the large map to see every detail, the barmaid pointed to its very centre and what was obviously a representation of the Martinborough Hotel in Memorial Square.

'We're here,' she said.

She then traced a line around the square and straight down Jellicoe Street onto Lake Ferry Road.

'Turn left there,' she said, pointing to the beginning of Dry River Road, 'and, well, a few kays down there on the right–' and here she pointed to a clever coloured drawing of a large winery complex of buildings and stainless steel vats surrounded by fields of grape-vines, planted in straight and unbroken rows, over all of which was printed a brand logo in black and yellow: *Faridale Farms, Wines of Martinborough, New Zealand, Founded 1898* '–and you can't miss it.'

Paul-Frank understood the barmaid's directions well enough – the map was clear and the route to Dry River Road was straight and uncomplicated – but it was a map of vineyards and wineries, not of houses. And so he asked: 'But–'

'Your Mrs Partridge was a Faridale, see,' said the barmaid. 'Rosie Faridale. I went to school with her and her sister.'

'I see,' said Paul-Frank who didn't see much at all but did manage to see at last how and why the Widow Partridge was so rich.

'The houses are about there,' said the helpful barmaid pointing to a spot two or three kilometres farther along Dry River Road from the winery. 'They're hidden behind some big old macrocarpa trees. A great long row of them. Up long drives. You'll find them if you look hard enough.'

'Them?'

Paul-Frank didn't understand the reference to plural houses.

'The Faridale girls' houses,' said the barmaid. 'Rosie and Pansy. They got a house each from their father. Or was it their grandfather?'

After receiving more information from the friendly and helpful barmaid, for which he gave thanks, Paul-Frank could see that it would be hard to get back to Faith and the others through the restaurant, which was now filling with diners, and the crowded bar, and so the barmaid told him to go out the side door onto Memorial Square.

'I'll tell your friends,' she said. 'You can meet them outside. It'll be easier.'

'Thanks for that.'

'No worries,' said the barmaid. And then, as she resumed her position behind the bar in the restaurant, which curved around into the public bar, he heard her call out loudly to the bar: 'They're going, everybody.'

And then, from the street, he could tell that the occupants of the bar had stopped whatever they were doing – that is, drinking and talking – and together were clapping loudly to salute the departure of the strange and sadly ignorant big-city foreigners.

'God that was embarrassing,' said Faith when they came together on the sunny street.

'Telling me,' said Paul-Frank.

'But do you know where to go, Pauly?' asked Faith anxiously.

Paul-Frank nodded but he looked rather perplexed. Faith could sense his confusion.

'Well, what's the problem?' she asked.

'I'll tell you later,' said Paul-Frank. 'Let's get the hell out of here.'

Chapter 25

'Blimmin hungry, love,' said Paul-Frank.

'Us too, Faith,' said Tatts McIndoe.

'I know,' said Faith sympathetically. 'It's getting late. I think we should get some lunch before we go any further.'

'Could go back to the pub,' said Paul-Frank.

'Choice kai in that pub,' said Ponytail. 'I smelled it, eh.'

'I don't want to go back there, Pauly,' said Faith. 'They were all laughing at us.'

They arrived at the parked Land Cruiser.

'Hang on,' said Faith, 'There was a nice little cafe just back there, around the corner. Seats outside and everything. Let's walk back there.'

And so the motley crew of five sat outside at the Village Café and shared two large pizzas with sweet iced coffee all round. And although the pizzas were delicious, and the sweet coffee as strong, cold and refreshing as anything they could get in Wellington, it was all consumed hungrily and hurriedly, without pleasure, merely as essential fuel to sustain them through whatever the rest of the afternoon might bring. And in the process Paul-Frank told Faith – told them all – what the old barmaid had told him: that Mrs Partridge had a sister called Pansy, that they were Faridales, that they had each inherited a large house on the Faridale estate when they inherited the entire Faridale wines business.

'You mean Mrs Partridge owns the whole Faridale thing?' asked Faith.

'Apparently,' said Paul-Frank. 'Her and her sister.'

'Which is how come she's so rich,' said Faith.

'Tolja,' said Ponytail.

'But she and her sister can't run a business as big as that,' said Faith. 'And anyway she lives in Wellington.'

'She's got lots of charities to do if you know what I mean,' chipped in Ponytail. 'And she's an official at The Lake.'

Faith and Paul-Frank ignored Ponytail; they were speaking to each other.

'Evidently there's a managing director, a chief winemaker and a board of directors, all appointed by her father to run the business for them,' said Paul-Frank. 'The lady in the pub told me. And there's a lot of blimmin staff. And seasonal staff too. Lots I think.'

Faith shook her head in amazement. This Mrs Partridge is obviously a very interesting woman, she thought.

'Better go,' she said.

Paul-Frank paid the bill and so, their stomachs filled and the male bladders emptied, they set off in the Land Cruiser around the square, past the big Four Square and down Jellicoe Street.

It was only a few minutes before they were in the Wairarapa countryside again, and only a few more minutes on the straight Lake Ferry Road before they reached Dry River Road on the left. The going on Dry River Road was straight and flat and it wasn't long before they passed the Faridale winery on the right, a virtual factory complex – Paul-Frank recognized it from the tourist map in the pub – surrounded by countless lines of grapes running like straight corn-rows across and up the north-facing sloping sides of the valley. Paul-Frank knew that the two Faridale houses must be farther on – a couple of kays more according to the barmaid at the hotel – but after more than just a few kilometres the road suddenly entered a shallow valley following what was once the winding bed of a long-gone river. Then it began climbing and winding into the hills; the straight and smooth sealed road from civilization became a grey and winding road to nowhere.

And there were sheep.

'Gone too far,' said Paul-Frank.

'How do you know?' asked Faith.

Paul-Frank pointed to a flock of sheep grazing on the dry grass in a hilly paddock on their left. And there was a wooden sign: "DAISYBANK" it said. "McGAFFIN BLOCK". And another sign with an arrow pointing across the road: "SHEEPYARDS".

'Sheep country,' said Paul-Frank. 'No grapes here.'

It wasn't easy to turn around the big Land Cruiser on the narrow road to nowhere but they were soon retracing their route with Paul-Frank's eyes watching the road while looking out now on the left for the large macrocarpa trees between which, according to the barmaid, he should find the hidden driveways; he was of course supported in his scrutiny by another four sets of keen eyes.

'Is that them?' asked Faith. 'Big macrocarpas, right?'

'Must be,' said Paul-Frank. 'How the blimmin heck did we miss them on the way in? Must be a hundred of them. A full kay's length or more.'

And so he slowed the car and they all concentrated on seeking a gap or two between the trees on the left which might be a driveway to one of the mysterious and virtually invisible

Faridale houses. But they eventually came to the other end of the row of dark trees.

'Stink!' said Ponytail, speaking for them all. 'Must be in there somewhere if you know what I mean.'

'Another go,' said Paul-Frank.

He turned the Land Cruiser around again, and again drove slowly along the long row of big macrocarpa trees now on the right. And even with their combined two old eyes, four middle-aged eyes and four young eyes scanning the edge of the road, seeking a gap between the trees that might be a driveway, they would surely have gotten to the other end without finding what they sought if a car hadn't lurched surprisingly and bumpingly onto the road from a gap in the trees ahead. It was an old red Toyota which the male driver, the only occupant, swerved sharply and leaningly into the road, straightened up, and sped urgently towards them, and past them, and thence, presumably, to the main road to Martinborough and beyond.

'He's blimmin travelling,' said Paul-Frank. 'Be stopped by the cops if he keeps that up.'

'Go up there,' said Faith urgently. 'Where he came out.'

The coarse gravel on the drive from Dry River Road to the house, through the hidden gap in the macrocarpa trees and then long and winding through the thick bush behind the trees, served as an excellent visitor alert and so Paul-Frank's Land Cruiser was heard by those inside the tall and handsome two-storied steep-roofed brick-and-tile house long before it turned into the concrete apron at the front door. There it stopped. It had to; there was nowhere else to go.

'Jeez!' said Paul-Frank. 'Look at that!'

'It's beautiful,' said Faith.

'Stee-yink!' said the sulking Ponytail from his low position in the back seat between the brothers.

'Farting hell, I aint never seen nothing like that before,' said Eric the Limp.

'I hate your language, brother,' said Tatts McIndoe, 'but I have to agree with your sentiment. It is indeed a remarkable sight.'

'And, stink some more!' exclaimed Ponytail again, unclipping his seat belt and rising now from the depths of his seat, anxious to quickly exit the Land Cruiser.

Chapter 26

Ponytail's first exclamation of surprise – surprise which was felt equally by the Land Cruiser's other four occupants – was caused by the sight which now filled their view through the Land Cruiser's windscreen: the back of a navy-blue Bentley, sparkling and gleaming in the afternoon sun, which appeared to spread its tasteful and shapely bulk heavily across the width of the concrete apron in front of the house.

'A blimmin brand new Bentley,' said Paul-Frank.

'It must belong to Mrs Partridge,' said Faith calmly.

Ponytail's second exclamation of surprise was caused by the presence of one of the four people now standing on the front porch in front of the open front door. They, the four people on the porch, had been warned of the Land Cruiser's arrival by the sound of its tyres on the gravel drive and were now waiting to greet their unexpected visitors. But it was not the Widow Partridge who surprised Ponytail (he knew she would be there), nor was it Simple Simon (although he didn't know he would be there), nor the young woman with him (whom he didn't even know). It was the presence of the fourth member of the welcoming party, dressed in a grey military-styled uniform which had surprised him so much.

'And stink some more,' he said. 'My cousin Willy. He must be the stinkin driver. I never knew that, eh.'

'Obviously he's Mrs Partridge's chauffeur,' said Faith calmly, 'by the uniform.'

'Chauffeur,' repeated Ponytail slowly as if tasting the word and finding it delicious. 'Chauffeur. That's it, eh. He's her stinkin chauffeur. What a choice job.'

The occupants of the Land Cruiser got out and moved to stand huddled together between its crudely angular front and the Bentley's wide rear. There they waited – like five nervous sheep in a pen – as the four people on the porch came down the four red concrete steps together and stood, unmoving, on the concrete path. It was an indescribably awkward moment for them all except perhaps for young Lucy Dixon who had no way of knowing the cognitive dissonance being experienced by the other eight people there, although each for a different reason.

Paul-Frank saw a man, a man as big and brawny as he, whom he had known only as Simple Simon, a petty crook, apparently a simpleton, who was once in his charge in Te Whareherehere prison; a man evidently thought capable of a brutal murder. But now that same simple-minded petty crook looked utterly normal, happy and carefree, standing there holding the hand of a pretty and equally normal and happy-looking young woman. And he saw not the Widow Partridge in the Widow Partridge, an official, irritating but tolerated visitor to Te Whareherehere, but a wealthy and kind-looking lady he would thereafter be compelled to refer to and address as Mrs Partridge.

Faith saw a woman she assumed to be the strange, rich and eccentric Widow Partridge.

'Is that her, Mrs Partridge?' she whispered to Paul-Frank who nodded his response without taking his eyes off the said lady.

Faith thought Mrs Partridge looked nice and kind and urbane, elegant and refined; rich, yes, but not at all strange or eccentric. And she seemed to be welcoming them with a smile.

And then she looked closely at the young woman who was standing with the big young man. She, the pretty young woman, looked vaguely familiar to Faith who was annoyed that she couldn't remember where she had seen her before. I *know* I've seen that face somewhere before, she thought. I'm sure it'll come to me later.

Ponytail firstly saw Willy, his cousin on his mother's side, the brother of Mrs Partridge's housekeeper Hinemoa. And then he was shocked to see that his friend Simon – whom everyone he knew called Simple Simon – looking far from simple and holding hands with that beautiful young woman. Who's that? wondered Ponytail confusedly. And what, he wondered further, was she and Simon doing at the Widow Partridge's house in Martinborough? And the Widow Partridge looked different somehow. So self-composed and self-assured. So rich. That's it, he thought. I knew she was rich but so rich, he thought. So stinkin Bentley-owning wine-growing rich. And at that moment he abandoned all thoughts of marriage to the Widow Partridge, fantastic as they always were anyway.

Tatts McIndoe and Eric the Limp were utterly flummoxed not only by being in the unfamiliar and intimidating openness of the Wairarapa countryside in which they now found themselves but also by the people facing them across the drive. Simple Simon was obviously not the same simple Simple Simon whom they had met at the front of the Metropolitan Cathedral of the Sacred Heart and of Saint Mary His Mother on Hill Street in Wellington (which now seemed so far away) on Christmas day (which now seemed so long ago); he didn't even look the same. And there was the Widow Partridge, a harmless, smiling and kind-looking old woman who had reminded them both – but Tatts McIndoe more – of their late Nan, to whom they had behaved so badly; they both felt utterly ashamed and wanted so much to apologise but couldn't find the words and were too afraid anyway to break the awkward silence.

Simon Partridge felt happy to be holding the hand of the woman he loved who had lately agreed to be his wife. Yet he was sad to see the dismay on the face of old Ponytail whom he had come to like with a kindly and protective fondness. He knew he had deceived the little fellow who had no idea that his friend Simple Simon was in fact what Ponytail would call "the long arm". Meanwhile he had nothing but contempt for the two young thugs – Big Ben's henchboys Tatts McIndoe and Eric the Limp – and wondered what they were doing there with Ponytail. Whatever it was all about he knew now for certain that his Uncle Aunty had been right: Detective Constable Simon Partridge's undercover career was over. And, finally, he was confused by the presence of the big man and the little woman who seemed to be with him; he thought he recognized the man from somewhere but couldn't remember where, and he had no idea why the two of them were there.

His mother was similarly confused. What on earth was poor old Ponytail doing with those two horrid young thugs, she wondered. And she had no idea who the little woman was – no idea at all – but like her son she thought the big man with the shaven head looked vaguely familiar. Still, it was her house, her home, and what enmity might once have existed between some of the parties there, at her place at that moment she felt she had a duty to welcome them all with Faridale courtesy. And so, after only a little hesitation, she smiled broadly, stepped forward, with her arms outspread, towards the group of five, standing nervously, uneasily, on the path between the big Land Cruiser and her Bentley, and said (because she couldn't think of anything else to say): 'Welcome to Faridale Farms, everyone. Now come inside and let's have a glass of wine and a talk and sort this all out.'

Of the five only Faith reacted while the others, including Paul-Frank, her own husband, stood where they were wishing, it would seem, that they were anywhere else. Faith though stepped forward confidently, smilingly.

'That'd be nice,' she said, holding out her hand. 'I'm Faith Ratanui.'

And so the two women shook hands and everyone relaxed and moved together to the front door of the big house.

Meanwhile, Detective Inspector Tim Glante was on his way back to Wellington with his precious cargo lying on the passenger seat beside him. A bit more than an hour later he was parking his little red Toyota in the Harris Street parking garage of the Wellington Central Police Station where, three floors up, Rembrandt Hawxwell was waiting for him, in his dimly lighted laboratory, together with two of his scientist colleagues. They had come in to work on this Sunday afternoon in response to Glante's special and urgent request.

'Got the bastard!' he said triumphantly (and loudly) as he threw open the door and entered Rembrandt Hawxwell's dark and quiet domain.

He handed the little black phone to the young scientist.

'Amazing,' said Hawxwell as he received it gingerly and held it carefully in one hand while he adjusted his spectacles with the other to take a close look.

'Take care of it,' said Glante, 'and duplicate everything it contains. Everything.'

'Can I listen?'

'No,' said Glante anxiously. 'Let's not risk dropping it or losing it or wiping it or deleting it or any bloody thing it. Copy it and then we'll all listen to it together.'

Hawxwell, the brilliant young genius and head of his department, handed the phone to an even younger woman genius standing at his side.

'This is Dixie O'Halloran,' said Hawxwell by way of introduction.

The serious-looking young woman in a bright white lab coat nodded silently at Glante who nodded silently back. And then she was gone from the gloomy room. Gone with the phone.

There was another man with Hawxwell; another young man with a demeanour much more jolly than Dixie O'Halloran's.

'This is Atticus Wright,' said Hawxwell. 'Detective Inspector Glante.'

The detective and the young man shook hands.

'He knows everything,' said Hawxwell. 'Sworn to secrecy.'

'Eh?' said Glante; he was taken aback.

'He did the make-up, Aunty,' said Hawxwell by way of explanation. 'He's an embalmer. The best in the country.'

'Hell, man?' said Glante, stepping back, surprised and genuinely impressed, and then stepping forward to shake the young man's hand again. 'A true *artiste*. An amazing job,' he added.

'A bit different,' said the young embalmer.

'She looked amazing. You'd never be able to tell,' insisted Glante. Then he held up both hands, flat, palms towards the embalmer. 'But no one must ever–'

'Don't worry, Mr Glante,' said Wright with a smile. 'I understand completely. But is she alright?' he added.

'Oh, shit yeah, she's fine and dandy,' said Glante. 'Saw her this morning when I got the phone. She's beaut. A bloody angel.'

'Oh, good,' said Wright. 'She was so nice you know. We really got on. I was sort of hoping–'

'Too late, mate,' said Glante quickly. 'My nephew Simon and her are, you know, like that.'

'Oh,' said Wright. He looked genuinely disappointed.

'Quick and the dead, mate,' said Glante. 'Pun intended.'

But Atticus Wright didn't laugh.

'But how about that fart though,' said Glante.

Hawxwell laughed. 'I told Atticus about that.'

But Atticus Wright didn't laugh again.

'Anyway, mate, I was right wasn't I?'

'About Big Ben?'

'Yeah. The dick, being the big dumb arse he is, saw the news, knew that Simon had piked out and thought someone else had done it and was taking the credit for his work. Couldn't stand it. Can you believe it?'

'You *were* right then,' said Hawxwell.

'Yeah. Skited his bloody mouth off and that little Ponytail shitbag did everything right just as he was told.'

'Everything?'

'No. Not quite everything I admit,' said Glante. 'Showing Big Ben that photo nearly gave it all away. Got stabbed for his trouble the silly little bastard.'

'Ouch,' said Hawxwell.

'But it doesn't matter now. It's all on the phone which means I've got the bastard, mate. I've got the bastard.'

Chapter 27

'An undercover cop. *Really*?' Max Bridlington was astonished.

He and Paul-Frank were sitting opposite each other having lunch in the court canteen. Toasted sandwiches. Ham, cheese and tomato. Hot. And cold chocolate milk.

'Really,' confirmed Paul-Frank. He picked up his sandwich and quickly put it down again. 'Ouch! Bit hot,' he said.

'Mine too,' said Max. 'I'll leave it a bit. Tenny-rate, you mean that Simple Simon's not simple at all?'

'Not a bit of it,' said Paul-Frank. 'Blimmin smart if you ask me. Just put it on. They sent him to The Lake and he pretended to be a dumb crook.'

'That's amazing,' said Max.

'Was there when I was there,' said Paul-Frank. 'Fooled me. Was there waiting when Big Ben got himself sent down on purpose.'

'So they got to know each other.'

'He got Big Ben's confidence,' said Paul-Frank. 'Great big bloke, just like Big Ben, so Big Ben thought he could strangle a girl and make it look like the Welly Alley Strangler. Paid him – or was going to pay him – five grand. Gave him half to start with.'

'And he thought that'd put Aunty off the trail.'

'Exactly,' said Paul-Frank.

'And they'd catch Simple Simon and he'd take the rap.'

'Big Ben wouldn't care about that.'

'No. You're right there,' said Max. 'Bit stupid of him though. Cops aren't that dumb. Aunty's certainly not. And even if Simple Simon really was simple and really did end up doing it why wouldn't he tell the police about getting paid to do it by Big Ben? And about all the others he didn't do? Big Ben must've been stupid.'

'Who said Big Ben was clever?' said Paul-Frank. 'I can tell you from experience, he's as blimmin thick as.'

'Crims really are so unbelievably stupid,' said Max.

'Agreed,' said Paul-Frank. He picked up his sandwich and took a hot buttery bite.

'And so you met the Widow Partridge properly at last,' said Max who tested his sandwich for heat before picking it up. 'And she turns out to be Simple Simon's mother.'

'They worked together,' said Paul-Frank when his mouth was free to speak. 'With Glante.'

'A family affair,' said Max before attacking his sandwich. 'Who'd have guessed all that?'

They didn't speak again until they had demolished their sandwiches and wiped their lips clean on a C and C serviette. They then pierced their boxes of chilled chocolate milk with the little pink plastic straw provided and began drawing up the cool, sweet and refreshing liquid.

Their conversation resumed between sips.

'So, a blimmin weird day altogether, Max, I tell you,' said Paul-Frank.

'And Simon's new girlfriend?' said Paul-Frank. 'Who was that?'

'Dunno really. Nice though,' said Paul-Frank. 'Actually blimmin gorgeous if you ask me. Lucy something. Faith thought she recognized her from somewhere but couldn't remember.'

'Yeah? So she's been hiding up there with him all this time?'

'Guess,' said Paul-Frank. 'Keeping him company I suppose.'

'Who else was there?'

'Mrs Partridge's chauffeur Willy,' said Paul-Frank remembering. 'Turned out that Willy and his sister Hine, Mrs Partridge's housekeeper, are actually Ponytail's cousins on his mother's side. From Tolaga Bay.'

'Small world,' said Max.

'He's like Ponytail,' said Paul-Frank. 'A crook she saved.'

'She sounds amazing,' said Max.

'She is,' said Paul-Frank. 'An amazing old bird. But, listen. It seems Willy's straight now, he and his sister have saved some money, they're going back to the East Coast, and guess what.'

'Go on,' said Max.

'Mrs Partridge gave Ponytail the chauffeur's job.'

'Wow. But will he be able to reach the pedals?'

Paul-Frank laughed and took a sip of his drink. 'And she's employed those two blimmin brothers at the winery,' he added.

'Doing what?' asked Max. 'They sound bloody hopeless to me.'

'They are,' said Paul-Frank. 'But I think she likes the idea of helping the blimmin hopeless. She reckons working outside in the fresh air all year'll build up their strength. Give them some good old Wairarapa health. And a tan maybe.'

'It's a funny story, Pauly,' said Max Bridlington. 'And that's it?'

'Well, Aunty had gone by then,' said Paul-Frank. 'He'd been there all morning. He came tearing out the drive just as we arrived.'

'How come?'

'Had the blimmin phone didn't he.'

'Oh, the phone.'

'Yeah,' said Paul-Frank. 'The phone. Ponytail's recording. Was there all the time in the house where Mrs Partridge posted it to Simon for safe keeping.'

'Why did he do that I wonder,' said Max. 'Big Ben I mean. Talk like that in The Lake? Tell everyone?'

'Like *you* told me,' said Paul-Frank. 'His type. Can't stand the idea of never being recognized.'

'That was my theory,' said Max. 'It's amazing that it came true like that.'

They were making gurgling bubbly finishing noises at the bottom of their boxes of chocolate milk when they were interrupted by the shambling figure of Detective Inspector Glante hovering over the end of their table. They put their empty milk boxes down and listened.

'I got the bastard,' said Glante, looking from one to other sitting on opposite sides of the table. 'Told you I would and I bloody did.'

'Good on you, Aunty,' said Max.

'You were there, at the house, after me, weren't you, Pauly,' said Glante.

Paul-Frank nodded. 'And my wife,' he said.

'And O'Gorman and those other two young dorks.'

'Yes,' said Paul-Frank hesitatingly, not knowing what the detective inspector was getting at.

'I should nick them all but, hell, they're not worth it,' said Glante. 'Now they're working for Rosie.'

'I know,' said Paul-Frank.

'Yeah. So you know all about Rosie Partridge, my sister-in-law, and her son Simon and what he does?'

'Suppose so,' said Paul-Frank.

'And Simon's girlfriend?'

'Met her,' said Paul-Frank. 'But I don't exactly *know* her.'

'Good,' said Glante. 'Better that you don't. They're getting married you know.'

'Gathered that,' said Paul-Frank.

'Well, all that you saw, all that you heard, all that you know,' said Glante, 'not a single bloody word, understand?'

Paul-Frank nodded dumbly. What was the big secret, he wondered. And why did this old cop always make him feel guilty for no reason?

'You too, Bridlington,' said Glante directly to Max.

'I get it, Aunty,' said Max breezily. 'Don't worry.'

'Right. Good,' said Glante apparently satisfied. Then he patted the left side of his baggy grey suit jacket with the flat of his right hand. 'Now I'm off to The Lake to charge one Benjamin Cedric Pye – aka the Welly Alley Strangler – with five murders. The bastard.'

'Good on you, Aunty,' said Max although Paul-Frank said nothing.

And then the usually weary-looking old detective – now evidently revitalized, re-energized, reinvigorated by his success – strode confidently out of the canteen, nodding his acknowledgments to this person and that, to his left and right, and thus out of the lives of Paul-Frank Ratanui and Max Bridlington, on his way to Te Whareherehere prison to discharge his last duty as a Detective Inspector of the Wellington police criminal investigation branch. And then: retirement.

'Five?' said Paul-Frank quietly. Quizzically. 'But who did the--'

'We better get going,' said Max, preoccupied with picking up his paper plate, serviette and empty pink-strawed chocolate milk box. 'Anyway, what did you say?'

'Oh, nothing,' said Paul-Frank as he collected up the debris of his own lunch. 'I was just thinking.'

– THE END –